# THE
# ONE
# AND
# ONLY

# THE ONE AND ONLY

*Sophie McKenzie*

Simon & Schuster

This edition published 2014

First published in Great Britain in 2009 by Simon and Schuster UK Ltd
A CBS COMPANY

1 3 5 7 9 10 8 6 4 2

Simon & Schuster UK Ltd
1st Floor
222 Gray's Inn Road
London
WC1X 8HB

Simon & Schuster Australia, Sydney
Simon & Schuster India, New Delhi

A CIP catalogue record for this book
is available from the British Library.

PB ISBN: 978-1-47112-152-4
EBook ISBN: 978-0-85707-669-4

Printed and bound by CPI Group (UK) Ltd, Croydon, CR0 4YY

www.simonandschuster.co.uk
www.simonandschuster.com.au

For Joe, my one and only

# 1

# Missing Eve

Nothing hurt like missing Eve.

My girlfriend had been gone two months and I still thought about her every day.

Eve's dad had shut her up in some convent school in Spain. He worked out there, running a hotel where we'd spent part of the summer holidays. He'd said she'd have to stay in the school for a term – no boys, no phones, no way of contacting the outside world. He did it because of me.

Because of us.

I wasn't supposed to know it was a convent school – with bars on the windows like a prison and a starchy brown uniform – but Eve's mum had told me.

It had taken me two weeks of going round every day to get any information out of her. Even then, she wouldn't tell me the things I really wanted to know.

Like, where *exactly* was Eve's school?

Had Eve said anything about me?

When was she coming home?

I think Eve's mum was scared I'd get on a plane and go out to Spain and rescue her. Believe me, I fantasised about doing just that all the time. But I had no idea where she was. And no money to get there, even if I did.

Of course what Eve's mum was most afraid of was what Eve's dad would do if he found out she'd told me anything.

Eve's dad. Jonno. A total bastard. The person I hated most in the whole world.

It was Bonfire Night. The fifth of November. I was going out later with my best mate, Ryan, and some other friends. There was just time for a quick visit to Eve's mum's house to see if there was any news.

I trudged resentfully up the path. I didn't expect things to be any different than they had been on my last visit, about ten days ago.

But they were.

Eve's mum had obviously been crying. Her eyes were all red and puffy when she opened the door. 'Hello, Luke.'

I shuffled awkwardly on the doorstep. I liked Eve's mum. For a start, she looked a lot like Eve. The same long blonde hair and heart-shaped face. And she was always nice to me. But I wished she wouldn't get so emotional about everything.

'Er . . . you all right, Mrs Ripley?'

'No. Not really.'

My chest tightened. 'Is it Eve? What's happened? What's the matter?'

'Her dad's saying she's got to stay out there for a *year.*' Her voice trembled. 'A whole year.'

'He can't!' I stared at her. 'It's only supposed to be until Christmas. That's what you agreed. You can't let him *do* this.'

Eve's mum twisted her hands together. 'How can I stop him? He's got all the money. And he is her father.'

*For goodness sake.*

Privately, I thought Eve's mum was more than a bit pathetic when it came to Jonno. OK, so he was big and loud and aggressive – and he owned her house and everything in it. But still – she could have moved out. Got a job. Supported herself and Eve. Even if it meant being a bit poorer.

'He's probably just trying to frighten you,' I said. 'Have you talked to Eve about it?'

I knew Eve and her mum spoke once a week. Eve's mum was too scared of Jonno to risk letting me talk to Eve myself. And she didn't say much about their conversations, but at least I knew Eve was still alive . . . still thinking about me.

'Eve thinks staying for the year's a good idea.'

'What?' A cold line of fear snaked its way down my spine.

'She said that now she's settled in it makes sense to finish out the year. That if she stays she'll be able focus properly on her art studies.'

I frowned. I couldn't believe Eve really thought this. Jonno had probably been visiting that day . . . listening to her conversation. Still.

'Did she say anything about . . . about . . . ?'

Eve's mum smiled sadly at me. 'About you?' She hesitated. 'Actually she did.'

'Well?' I dug my hands deep into my pockets, hands clenched into fists.

Eve's mum sighed. 'She said the two of you should forget about each other.'

*What?* 'I don't believe you.'

'I'm not saying she meant it, Luke,' Eve's mum sniffed. 'She might have been saying it because she knew it was what her dad'd want to hear. But it's what she said. That it was stupid you both waiting about for a whole year. That you should move on.'

I nodded, thinking it through. I was sure Eve was just trying to convince her dad she was over me. Well, I was *almost* sure. My stomach twisted. Maybe what she'd said

4

was what she really thought. It was unbearable not being able to talk to her myself.

I refused Eve's mum's offer of a drink and wandered off to the park, where I was meeting Ryan and the others. This nagging feeling that Eve had never made that much effort to stand up for herself against her dad had been worming through me for weeks. Now it forced its way to the front of my mind.

*How can you be happy to stay in Spain for a whole year, Eve? If it was me, nothing would stop me getting back here to you. Nothing. Don't you want me any more? You didn't even call me on my sixteenth birthday. That was September, Eve. Now it's November. Where* are *you?*

I walked through the trees at the entrance to the park. The wind was ice cold. Fierce. People all around me were tugging at their jackets to keep themselves warm.

*Surely there's some way you could get in touch with me, Eve? Even if the school doesn't allow mobiles, it certainly has phones. And there must be a networked computer somewhere. Anyway, how hard could it be to borrow a stamp and get one of the other girls at the school to take a letter to a postbox for you?*

I could see the top of the massive bonfire at the other end of the park. It glowed orange above the silhouettes of all the people standing, staring at the flames.

*Have you met someone in Spain?*

No. That couldn't be it. Jonno would hardly separate her from me and let her mix with other guys. I walked past the small pond where Eve and I had met up all through February half-term, when she was still going out with Ben.

*So what then? Is it that you just don't feel the same any more?*

The ground was littered with twigs and leaves from the trees above my head. I crunched across them, trying to reassure myself.

*I'm not going to jump to conclusions. OK? It was like your mum said. You were saying what Jonno wanted to hear. Weren't you, Eve?*

I had jumped to conclusions in the summer – over this Spanish guy. Eve had been in his room one night. She'd said nothing had happened but I hadn't believed her. Then it turned out he was gay and miserable about not being 'out' with his family and they had just been talking after all. Eve dumped me for not trusting her. The next few days until I got her back were hell.

I wasn't going to make that mistake again. And yet . . . it was hard to feel OK without any reassurance.

I could hear, as well as see, the big bonfire now. Hissing and spitting and crackling. Little kids were running about with sparklers, writing their names in the air. There was a square fence made of metal barriers set several metres away from the fire, surrounding it. People were pressed up against the metal bars, staring at the flames in the centre.

I stared too, admiring the way the fire licked and leaped, always moving, eating at the logs beneath it, twisting up into the sky.

I couldn't see Ryan or any of our friends, so I pushed my way through the crowd to get closer to the barrier. The heat from the fire was strong on my face, even at this distance. And then I felt a different heat. The sensation that someone was staring at me. I looked round. A girl I hadn't noticed before was standing next to me. As I met her eyes, she smiled.

She was pretty – with a small, round face and a dimple in her chin. And she had amazing hair – great waves of red curls that tumbled right the way down her jacket. The flames from the bonfire were lighting the curls, creating a golden halo effect around her head as if the hair itself was on fire.

'Hi,' she said.

I frowned. Did I know her? She *looked* familiar. Yes, I was sure I'd seen her before. But not at school. Somewhere else. With someone else I knew well.

'Haven't I met you before?' I said.

The girl's smile deepened, revealing two more dimples in her cheeks. 'That has to be the cheesiest line ever,' she said.

'It's not a line,' I said, feeling myself blushing. 'I wasn't . . . I didn't . . . I mean, I really thought I'd seen you somewhere.'

I turned awkwardly back to the fire.

*God, Eve. See how crap I am without you?*

'Oh.' I sensed the girl was still looking at me.

I stared at the fire, wanting to walk away, but feeling it would look rude.

'I'm sorry,' the girl said. She leaned forwards on the barrier, next to me.

I glanced down at her. She grinned.

'Luke! Hey, Luke, man.' Ryan raced over. 'Where've you been? Come on, this is rubbish. We're going down the Burger Bar.'

He punched me on the shoulder. Then he turned towards the girl. 'So who've you been chat— OH MY GOD. HAYLEY.'

'Ryan.' The girl's eyes were wide. The hiss of the fire and the low murmur of people chatting filled the silence.

Then Ryan stepped forward. With characteristic swagger he wrapped his arms around the girl and hugged her.

'Hey, where've you been, Hayley?' he said, twisting round to wink at me over the girl's shoulder. 'You just dropped off the face of the earth.'

The girl pulled away from him, making an obvious

effort not to smile. 'Actually *you're* the one who dropped off the face of the earth. After that party in February.'

'Oh, right.' Ryan looked sheepish. 'Sorry.' He gave her what I knew was his most charming grin. 'I must have been mad,' he said.

Hayley rolled her eyes. 'Yeah, right. I heard you started going out with some girl – Chloe somebody?'

It all fell into place.

'You were at our party,' I said. *'That's* where I remember seeing you.'

*Leaving with Ryan and him snogging your face off at the end of our road.*

Ryan and Hayley both turned to me.

'D'you remember Luke from then?' Ryan said. 'Chloe's his sister.'

Hayley stared at me.

'Hey, d'you wanna come with us down the Burger Bar?' Ryan said.

I watched Hayley. I really didn't care whether she came or not.

*You see, Eve? I only care about you.*

Hayley's face fell. 'I can't. I'm with my parents and my sister. We're going out for dinner at this really expensive restaurant. It's a great place, but . . .' She tailed off.

Ryan shrugged. 'No problem.'

Hayley hesitated. 'Maybe another time though.' She glanced at me, then back to Ryan. 'You know? Let me know if there's a good party on or whatever, yeah? Um . . . have you still got my number?'

Ryan grinned at her. 'Here.' He handed her his mobile. 'Put it in my phone. Next time I hear of a "good party" I'll call you.'

Hayley blushed as she punched in her number. She said goodbye quickly and scampered away.

As we wandered over to where our friends were standing, Ryan started writing a text. I peered over his shoulder. He was calling up Hayley's number.

'What are you doing?' I said. 'You can't call her straight away. In fact, you can't call her at all. What about Chloe?'

Ryan grinned at me. 'I'm just forwarding her number to you, you idiot. That's why she gave it to me.'

I stared at him. '*What?*'

'Lu- uke, man.' Ryan rolled his eyes. 'Didn't you see the way she looked at you? You should ask her out. One date's not going to hurt anyone.'

As he strolled away from me, my mobile beeped. I checked the text. There was Hayley's number next to a message from Ryan.

TLKS A LOT BUT FIT BDY. CALL HER.

# 2

# Staying in

We had an OK time at the Burger Bar – then Ryan went off to meet Chloe and the other guys disappeared with their girlfriends or went to crash a party.

I decided to go home early.

I knew I wouldn't call Hayley. Don't get me wrong, she was pretty – and I'm not made of stone. If there'd been some way of getting off with her without having to speak to her first, I'd probably have been tempted. Especially now, after what Eve had said. But I couldn't face the idea of talking to her. Of having to go on some date and pretend to be interested in her and her life.

Ryan hadn't understood at all, especially when I told him about Eve. I got the distinct impression he thought I'd been dumped and should react by going out with as many girls as possible.

'Best way to pick yourself up, Luke,' he said, 'is to go out and have some fun.'

I shook my head. It struck me that Ryan and I were total opposites. He loved flirting with girls. He would go to a party and chat up everyone there – but he always somehow ended up with Chloe. Whereas, if I couldn't have Eve I cared far less about who I ended up with, I just didn't want to have to do all that exhausting talking first.

'Maybe you could warm them up for me, then pass them on,' I'd said, only half joking.

Does that sound mean? Maybe it was. But it was all – only – because of Eve. If she'd been there I would have talked to her, listened to her, waited as long as she wanted for the chance to hold her and kiss her and . . .

*Oh God.*

I let myself in at our front door and headed up the stairs to my room. I could hear Mum yelling in the kitchen. *Bloody hell.* Were she and Chloe *ever* going to stop shouting at each other?

I stopped, halfway up the stairs. Chloe wasn't here. Ryan had been going off to meet her.

'Of *course* everything's going to change.' Mum sounded like she was crying.

The kitchen door crashed open and Matt stormed across the hall below me.

'I don't see why it has to,' he shouted.

Matt's my mum's boyfriend, the father of her soon-to-be-born baby. They haven't been together that long – about ten months. And he doesn't live with us, thank goodness.

He wormed his way into Mum's life after my dad died in January.

He was Dad's best friend.

I hate him.

Mum's voice echoed plaintively out from the kitchen. 'Please, Matty. Please.'

Matt looked back as he opened the front door. He caught sight of me on the stairs. 'It's just a baby,' he shouted, glaring straight at me. 'I don't see why kids have to take over your life.'

I stuck a finger up at him. He made a face, then walked out, slamming the door shut behind him.

Mum emerged from the kitchen in tears. She looked up and saw me.

'Oh, Luke, I'm sorry you had to hear that.' She tried to smile. 'I don't know why he gets so angry.'

I walked back downstairs, my head pulsing with fury.

*Stupid bastard. How dare he upset her like that.*

I put my arms round Mum and hugged her. She hugged me back, then wiped her eyes.

'He's just got so impatient with me recently. All I'm trying to do is help him prepare for . . . for the baby coming. But he acts as if me getting pregnant has somehow made me a completely different person.' She sighed. 'D'you think I've changed, Luke?'

I shrugged, feeling awkward. I hate it when Mum wants to talk about stuff like that. In fact, she *had* changed massively in the past few months. For a start it took her ages to do anything or walk anywhere. And she looked completely different too. All fat-faced. Fat everywhere, really. I knew it was just the baby – but it was weird seeing it.

'A bit, maybe. I dunno, Mum.' I turned back to the stairs, wondering how many more middle-aged women in tears I was going to have to deal with tonight. Immediately I felt guilty.

I turned back. 'You OK, Mum?'

I desperately wanted her to say yes, that she was fine. I glanced up the stairs towards my room – where I could close the door and shut out everything else . . . where I could play music and think about Eve.

'Course I'm OK.' She smiled. 'I just miss your dad.'

We looked at each other.

'Me too,' I said.

I did miss him. Especially now, without Eve.

'I'm going to call Trisha,' Mum said. 'See if she can come round.'

I breathed a sigh of relief. 'Good idea.'

Trisha was Mum's friend. Her best friend really. They hadn't known each other that long. Mum had met her at some ante-natal clinic. Trisha was pregnant too. She was divorced, with a three-year-old daughter. She and Mum really hit it off. They were always getting together, giggling over, like, one glass of wine, telling themselves how naughty they were to be drinking at all.

I liked Trisha. She treated me like a grown-up, which was more than any of Mum's other friends ever had. Mum had fallen out with most of them when she started seeing Matt. They all said it was too soon after Dad died. Then when she got pregnant it was the final straw. I overheard a couple of them talking once, saying Mum was like a teenager – really irresponsible.

That pissed me off. Why does everyone think teenagers are automatically irresponsible? I mean, it wasn't like I'd got *my* girlfriend pregnant.

*Yeah right, Luke. Get real. You weren't even having sex.*

I gritted my teeth and carried on walking up the stairs.

Several weeks passed. The weather got colder. Mum got fatter. Matt came round less and less. And Ryan kept nagging me to call Hayley.

'Eve's going to be away for a whole year,' he kept saying. 'You can't live like a pigging monk.'

Even Chloe joined in.

'I think you're being a bit of an idiot,' she said. 'Even if Eve still wants to go out with you when she's back, I'm sure she'd understand you going on a date. I mean, she wouldn't expect you to stay in *all* the time.'

I shrugged. I'd been round to see Eve's mum a couple of times since Bonfire Night. She'd said Eve had sounded happier since she'd decided to accept staying on for the whole year. She also said Eve kept insisting I should forget her. Get on with my life.

There was no way I could know if she was telling the truth. No way I could know what Eve really felt.

It was horrible.

Then, at the beginning of the final week of term, in the middle of a freezing cold, dark December, Chloe dropped a bombshell that put Eve out of my head for almost an entire evening.

'I'm moving out,' she said.

We were eating tea together. It was one of the few occasions Mum had managed to get the three of us to sit round the table this year. Usually Chloe just came and went as she pleased. So I'd been surprised when she'd joined us. Now I saw why.

'What are you talking about?' Mum snapped.

I chewed slowly on a mouthful of lasagne.

16

'I've got a job,' Chloe said nonchalantly. 'In a shop in town. Starts on Sunday. So I'm leaving school. And I'm moving into this house-share in South London. It's this girl's parents' house. They own lots of places – rent them out. But because it's her, the rent's dead cheap.'

Mum's mouth dropped open. 'What about school? You can't just leave home like this. It's—'

'Perfectly legal,' Chloe smirked. 'I'm seventeen. I can do what I like.'

'No you can't.' Mum thumped the table. Her face was bright red. 'Chloe, this is so typical. You cannot just—'

'Don't tell me what I can and can't do!' Chloe shouted.

I stood up and took my plate up to my room.

I could hear their voices all the way up the stairs and through the walls and door of my bedroom. I sat down on the bed. There was no point Mum yelling like that. I knew from experience that Chloe was going to do whatever she wanted. Nothing and no one would stop her. Well. Maybe one person might.

A few minutes later I heard Chloe stomp up the stairs. I darted out onto the landing and caught her as she was going into her room.

'Does Ryan know?'

'Of course.' Chloe tried to shut her door. I pushed my foot against it, forcing it open.

Chloe swore at me.

'Doesn't he mind?' I said. 'If you're on the other side of London you won't see each other so much.'

*I'd mind, if it was us, Eve. I'd mind.*

'Piss off, Luke. No, he doesn't mind. He thinks it'll be great for me.'

I stared at her. Then I moved my foot out of the way and she slammed the door shut in my face.

I talked to Ryan about it the next day at school. He was as relaxed about the idea of Chloe moving away as she had been.

'It makes sense, Luke. She hates school. And you know your mum does her head in. Anyway, we'll still see each other at weekends.'

I didn't understand them. How could they not mind the idea of being more apart? Mum wasn't bothered about that, of course. She just kept going on about Chloe throwing away her education.

'She should be going to university, Luke,' she kept saying. 'She's so bright. She got great GCSE grades. She's just wasting her talents.'

But Mum might as well have saved her breath. Chloe had everything planned and nothing was going to stand in her way. She decided to move out the day after term ended – a Saturday. She and Ryan and loads of our friends were going out to this new club in town the night before.

'You gotta come, Luke,' Ryan told me. 'It's a new place. It'll be a whole new experience.'

And it was. Though not exactly in the way Ryan meant.

# 3

# Hayley

Our fake ID worked like a charm. The club was heaving. The music was great. The atmosphere was buzzing. Everyone was in a good mood. Even I was enjoying myself.

I was standing at the bar, watching Chloe and some of her friends dancing in their sexy club gear. They were making fun of the group of girls next to them . . . copying their moves. The other girls hadn't even noticed. I laughed as Chloe waved her arms above her head and made a silly face.

Despite her moods and the way she was always arguing with Mum, I was going to miss her. Ryan wandered over and stood beside me, watching them too.

'Are you really cool with her going?' I shouted over the music.

Ryan smiled into his beer. 'Course I am. It's what she's gotta do. Anyway, we've talked about it. We decided it was the right time to take a break anyway.'

'Take a break?' I stared at him. How could he sound so laid back? 'You mean split up?'

'Not exactly. More like just saying we could see other people too.'

'See other people?' I said.

Ryan grinned. 'Is there an echo in here? Look, Luke, I know you're all heavy about Eve and stuff, but it's not like that for everyone. Chloe and I've decided. We're both too special not to share round a bit.'

His grin deepened.

I shrugged and turned back to watch Chloe and her friends.

*Whatever, Ryan. Whatever works for you.*

A few moments later a high-pitched, girly squeal sounded over the top of the music. I turned to see Ryan flinging his arms round a girl with a mass of red, curly hair. The bonfire girl. In high heels and an extremely tight dress.

'Hayley, you made it,' Ryan shouted.

Hayley disentangled herself, checking the little glittery clips in her hair were still in place. She smiled shyly across at me. 'Hi,' she said.

'Hi.' I glanced at Ryan.

'Luke begged me to invite you,' Ryan grinned.

I frowned. *Jesus, Ry.* 'Er . . .'

Ryan whacked me on the arm. 'Ooops. Sorry, man.' He winked at Hayley. 'Guess I'll leave you two alone together.'

He sloped off towards the girls on the dance floor.

*Thanks a million, Ryan.*

Hayley smiled again. 'D'you want a drink?' she said.

'Cool. Thanks.' I watched her lean against the bar, trying to attract the barman's attention.

It didn't take long.

Ryan had been right about the hot body. Hayley's dress was so tight I could see every curve as I followed her outline all the way down. *God.* She had the fittest bum . . . And *she* was buying *me* a beer!

I decided to talk to her.

'So how d'you meet Ry?' I shouted over the music.

Hayley handed me a bottle of beer. 'At the cinema. I was with some friends and he just came over and started talking to me.' She grinned at me, her cheeks dimpling. 'You know what he's like.'

I nodded. Ryan. The world's most successful flirt.

'So you went out?' I said.

Hayley sipped her beer. 'Yeah. Only a couple of times, though. One of those times was your party. But I didn't see him after that. We . . . it wasn't a big deal. You know?' She stared up at me meaningfully.

'Whatever,' I said hurriedly. The last thing I wanted her to think was that I was interested.

*Why not be interested?* said a small voice in my head. *Eve doesn't want you any more.* I took a swig of beer. 'This is a good place, isn't it?'

Hayley nodded. 'Yeah. Though I went to this really flash club last week which was better. Cost a fortune to get into.'

I didn't know what to say to that. I tried to think back to the Six Steps Ryan had told me about.

*Six Steps to get you any girl.*

I sighed. Who cared about steps to a girl. I'd had a girl. The perfect girl.

*What are you doing now, Eve? Are you thinking about me?*

'I can't stay long here, though.' Hayley's voice brought me back to the noisy room.

'What?' I shouted.

'I've got to check on the fish in my sister's flat,' Hayley explained.

*What was she talking about?*

There was a long pause.

Then Hayley spoke again. 'I think I'll go and dance.' She looked at me expectantly. The words 'me too' stalled in my throat, like a crap car.

I watched her high-heel her way onto the dance floor, then I turned round and slumped against the bar. Why was I so rubbish with girls?

*It was easy with you, Eve. Why aren't you here?*

I stared down at my beer. The music thudded in my head. I'd never felt lonelier in my life.

Ryan materialised at my elbow. 'What's the matter?' he said. 'You're not blowing Hayley out are you?'

I ran my hand through my hair. 'I just can't talk to her,' I said. 'I don't know what to say.'

Ryan rolled his eyes. 'Believe me,' he said. 'You don't need to say much. I guarantee she's not interested in your conversation.'

I stared at him.

'I told you already,' Ryan said, exasperated. 'She likes talking. She likes you. Just listen. Then go for it.'

He vanished, dragged onto the dance floor by one of Chloe's friends.

I wandered round the club for a while. Everyone else seemed to be having a great time, but all the fun had evaporated for me. I hated myself for feeling so rubbish.

*Snap out of it, Luke. You're being stupid.*

Maybe I should try talking to Hayley again. I looked round for her. And suddenly, as if by magic, she was there, right beside me.

'Hi.' I smiled. 'I was looking for you. I owe you a beer.'

Her eyes sparkled up at me. 'I have to go,' she said.

'Oh,' I said. 'Oh . . . OK.'

Hayley hesitated a second. 'D'you want to come with me?'

'What?' I said. 'To the fish-care flat?'

She grinned. 'Yeah. It's not far. In fact it would be nice to go with someone. I get a bit freaked out in the dark on my own.'

I nodded. I knew what that felt like from the night that Eve's ex, Ben, had beaten me up. I drained my drink.

'Sure,' I said. 'I'll come with you.'


The flat was about twenty minutes' walk away.

Hayley talked most of the way there. 'It's not really my sister's flat,' she said. 'It's her boyfriend's. He's only twenty-one but he's loaded. He bought her this dress I'm wearing. She only wore it once then she let me have it. She does that with loads of stuff – make-up and jewellery and . . .'

I tuned out completely. It was a cold night and our breath was misting in front of our mouths. I glanced down from time to time, snatching glimpses of Hayley's bum and legs. She had this slightly strutting way of walking which was really sexy.

We stopped outside a modern-looking brick apartment

25

block. Hayley fumbled with a key and we were inside. The hall was laid with a soft grey carpet and the walls were painted pale green.

We crossed the hall. Hayley pressed the button for the lift. After talking all the way here, she suddenly seemed self-conscious.

'So what's with these fish you've got to check on?' I said.

'My sister's boyfriend keeps tropical fish,' Hayley said. 'Some of them are worth a fortune. When he goes away he sets up this automatic feeder thing, but he likes it being checked. That's partly why I've got the keys. They're away until tomorrow night, so . . . so I thought I should check on it . . . on the fish . . .'

The lift door opened and we stepped inside.

'You mean you've come round in the middle of the night just to check whether his fish-feeding system is working?'

Hayley pressed the button for the seventh floor. She looked at the lift carpet.

It suddenly occurred to me that the whole fish-checking scenario might have been a cover for getting me to leave the party with her.

'Oh,' I said.

We ascended to the seventh floor in silence.

# 4
# Temptation

The flat was a total shag pad, complete with plain wooden floors, massive soft leather sofas and an enormous plasma screen TV. Windows ran all the way round two of the walls. They overlooked the river and the centre of London, all lit up with street lamps and Christmas lights.

'Wow.' I looked round. 'Cool place.'

Hayley took off her jacket and wandered over to an enormous fish tank in the corner. A handful of brightly-coloured fish were swimming happily through green fronds and bubbling blue water.

The feeder system was obviously working fine.

'What does your sister's boyfriend do?' I said, genuinely curious about how someone so young could afford a place like this.

'He's in the City,' Hayley says. 'Earns masses. The furniture in here cost a fortune – it's all designer stuff. That glass table's worth over ten thousand pounds. He's got this amazing sports car, too. I've been out in it. It cost him, like, seventy grand . . .'

I tuned out again, remembering Alejandro's Alfa Romeo Spider and the night he'd driven me out in it in Mallorca. When he'd told me that Eve loved me and still wanted to go out with me.

*Is that still what you want, Eve?*

I wandered across the room to a large modern print on the wall. Eve had a similar picture on a postcard in her bedroom.

Something constricted in my chest.

*I wish you could see this. You'd love it.*

'That's an original,' Hayley said confidently. 'Worth a packet.'

It struck me that Hayley not only talked a lot – as Ryan had said – but that she was also completely obsessed with how much everything cost.

I suddenly missed Eve unbearably. Maybe I should just go home. Although . . .

I turned round. Hayley was looking at me from one of the windows on the other side of the room. Her face was lit up with excitement, her eyes shining with how fantastic the flat was and how much she was enjoying showing it off to me.

'It's a great place,' I said. 'I'd love to live somewhere like this.'

We stared at each other. She was undeniably hot. Not Eve hot. But her face was pretty. And she had a great body.

*Go and kiss her. She wants you to kiss her. And stop thinking about Eve.*

Hayley shrugged. 'Maybe you will some day.'

I wandered over to her, my heart beating fast. Hayley turned away to look out of the window. 'It's a great view, isn't it?' she said.

I reached out and touched her cheek, turning her face back to me. I gazed into her eyes. 'Amazing view,' I said.

OK. I *know* that was super-cheesy. A real 'line'. But it worked. Her eyes sort of melted up at me. I leaned down and kissed her.

I hadn't kissed anyone since the night on the beach when I'd said goodbye to Eve. Those kisses had been sad and gentle and full of love. This was completely different. Hayley was snogging me as hard as I was snogging her, her small tongue flicking against my mouth. I reached round and ran my hands right down her back. Eve had loved it when I did that.

After a few moments, Hayley pulled away from me. Her face was slightly flushed as she blew out her breath. 'Wow. Who taught you to kiss like that?'

*Eve.*

Shit. *Stop it, Luke. Stop thinking about her.*

I shrugged.

'I wasn't sure if you liked me,' Hayley looked shyly up at me. 'I mean, if you knew I . . .' She blushed. 'Um . . . d'you want a drink?'

'Sure.'

She led me across the living room and into the little kitchen area – all clear, steel surfaces. Hayley pulled open the deep freezer drawer at the bottom of the enormous fridge. It was empty apart from a frozen pizza and a bottle of vodka. She took out the vodka and filled two little shot glasses to the brim.

We sipped at them, staring at each other across the kitchen.

I still couldn't think of a single thing to say to her. In fact, the only thing on my mind was kissing her again. But before I could make a move, she smiled.

'I haven't finished showing you round,' she said.

She knocked back the rest of her drink, then walked out of the kitchen area. I downed my own glass, feeling the syrupy vodka burn through me. Then I turned and followed her.

'There's the bathroom,' she said. I glanced through the door, catching a glimpse of toffee-coloured marble.

'And here . . .' Hayley pushed open the door opposite. It was a bedroom. More stunning views over the city. Big black wood furniture. And an enormous steel-frame bed covered with white sheets.

Hayley leaned against the door frame. I smiled, then kissed her again. *Mmmn.* I ran my hand down the side of her dress. *God, was she sewn into it?* It was stretched like a skin over her whole body.

Her whole, fit, curvy body.

We snogged for a few minutes.

Hayley was kissing like she really meant it. *Go on. Next stage. Next stage.* After a minute I risked bringing my hands round to the front of her dress.

*Oh yes.*

Hayley was holding me tighter. Kissing me harder. *Yes. Yes. Yes. Yes.* I steered her across to the bed, then pulled her down beside me. We stared at each other for a second. There was something in the way she was looking at me.

My heart hammered. This instinct I hardly dared trust was telling me that if I kept going, she wouldn't stop me. *Trust it. Go on.*

I slipped the strap of her dress down over her shoulder. *All right.* I could hear myself gasping as I reached round for the zip and pulled it down. Suddenly the dress was loose in my hands, her skin smooth and soft under my fingers. I watched her face, half expecting her to tell me to zip the dress back up.

But she didn't.

She just rolled away from me and peeled herself out of it completely. *Whoa*. She laughed at the expression on my face, then turned away and hung the dress carefully over a chair. Somehow I got my own clothes off and then she was back, lying down beside me, smiling. Inviting.

This was *it*. This was only freakin' *it*.

We started kissing again. *Jesus*. She was making little moaning sounds as I touched her. It was like a dream. All happening so fast. No one would believe it. Ryan's face – all impressed – flashed in front of my eyes. *Yes. It's going to happen*. Except. *Shit*.

I lay on top of her and pushed her hair back from her face.

'Have you . . . ?' I faltered. 'I mean, have you . . . ?'

'Yeah, several times.' Hayley murmured. 'It's OK.'

I could feel myself blushing. 'I didn't mean that. I meant have you got . . . you know . . . it's just I didn't bring . . . I mean . . .'

Hayley wriggled out from underneath me and reached across to the side of the bed. She pulled open a drawer, drew out a pack of condoms and looked back at me.

'That's sweet,' she whispered. 'Sweet you didn't assume.'

I stared at the condoms, a stab of fear thrilling deliciously through my totally sexed-up head.

Hayley's eyes widened. 'This is your first time, isn't it?' she said.

My face reddened again. I couldn't look at her.

Hayley wriggled back underneath me and put her arms round my neck. 'Luke?'

*Be cool.*

I stared down at her. She raised her eyebrows and gave me this mocking, sexy smile. 'So. You OK with this?'

*Was I OK with it?*

*Was she serious?*

I'd been OK with it since we'd kissed by the window. I'd been desperate to get OK with it for at least three years – ever since I first started properly imagining this moment.

And yet this was absolutely not what I'd expected to happen tonight. With this girl I hardly knew. And here. In this designer flat. On this big, designer bed.

Of course, at the time I didn't think any of that.

I just thought one thing.

Yes. *Oh, yes, please.*

# 5

# Do what you have to do

I didn't get home until nearly six am. I left Hayley asleep in the flat and caught one of the first tubes back to North London. It was freezing cold and still dark outside, but I was so pleased with myself that I hardly noticed.

I was all in my head, reliving the last few hours.

It didn't even occur to me to feel guilty that I'd stayed out all night until I was walking down our front path. With a jolt I remembered how worried Mum had been back in March, when I hadn't got back from a party until after three am. As I turned my key in the lock I prayed that she'd gone to sleep long before my getting-home time. She usually did these days.

The house felt cold and still. I shut the door softly and listened for a moment. *Good.* No sounds.

And then Ryan walked out of the kitchen. He was still wearing his clubbing clothes and he looked exhausted – his face was far paler than normal and his eyes all strained.

We stared at each other.

'What are you doing here?' I said.

'Your mum's having her baby,' he said shortly. 'Where the hell have you been?'

'The baby?' What was he talking about. 'I thought it wasn't due 'till next year.'

'It wasn't.' Ryan yawned. 'It's about a month early.'

My heart skipped a beat. 'Is Mum OK?'

'Far as we know. Luke, what happened to you? Chlo and I got back here at about two and your mum was in pain and crying, but saying over and over she was fine – and Matt was shouting at her. So Chloe started yelling at him.' He rolled his eyes. 'Then Matt took your mum to the hospital. She didn't want Chloe to come, so Chloe got completely hysterical. I managed to get her to go to bed about four am – she's supposed to start her new job tomorrow, which is now today, but she made me promise to stay awake in case Matt called.' Ryan yawned again and beckoned me into the kitchen. 'I was just making a tea. D'you want one?'

I nodded and followed him into the kitchen.

'Why didn't you answer your phone?' Ryan said, plopping a teabag into a mug for me. 'We called you every fifteen minutes between about two and four.'

I thought back to what I was doing between two and four and how my switched-off phone had been lying beside my clothes on the floor of Hayley's sister's boyfriend's bedroom.

I sat down at the table and ran my hands through my hair. 'So was Mum worried about me?'

Ryan shook his head. 'She was too freaked with the pain and coping with Matt and then Chloe in floods of tears. Chloe's been worried though. Not that she admitted it.' He brought two mugs of tea over to the table and sat down, yawning again. Then his eyes narrowed. 'So was it Hayley? I noticed she'd gone after I realised you had. I wasn't sure but . . .'

I looked away.

Ryan thumped the table with delight. 'All right! I told you she was hot. God, I'm good. I should charge a fee. So how far d'you get?'

My cheeks burned.

'Oh. My. God.' Ryan sucked in his breath. 'No way. Whoa. You lucky . . . I *thought* you looked different.'

I looked up at him. 'Different?'

Ryan grinned. 'Yeah. Like a cat who's just drunk three saucers of cream or something. Like . . . like . . . really satisfied.'

I stared at him. Ryan was amazing. How did he always *know*? Then I realised something. For the first time since I'd met him, Ryan sounded impressed.

'So go on,' he said.

I told him – a (mostly) truthful summary of what we'd done and how up for it all Hayley had been – enjoying the way he hung on every word, his eyes wide and eager to hear it all.

I got to the part where I'd slipped out of the flat leaving Hayley asleep and sat back, sipping my tea.

'Wow.' Ryan shook his head. 'She'd never have done all that with me,' he said. Then he looked me in the eyes. 'What about Eve?'

Her name was like a slap in the face. The truth was, I'd been trying not to think about Eve at all for the past few hours.

'What about her?' I glared at Ryan. 'This doesn't make any difference. It just happened. There's no reason why Eve even has to know about it. Anyway, you were the one who kept insisting I should get off with Hayley. "Just listen. Then go for it." That's what you said.'

'I didn't think you'd get the chance to go for *all* of it.' Ryan laughed. 'So, you gonna see her again, man?'

I shook my head. I'd already thought about that on the way home. Hayley was OK and she looked good, but I couldn't imagine going out with her. All she ever seemed to talk about was her clothes and the stuff in the flat and how expensive it all was. The truth was I didn't really like her very much. No. That wasn't quite right. I did like her, as far as I felt anything at all. It was more that I didn't really care about her. When I thought about what we'd just done together, it didn't seem to have much to do with her. Still. Maybe sex was always like that.

'Well that's typical boy, that is,' sneered a voice from the door.

I spun round. Chloe was staring at both of us from the kitchen doorway.

'You shag the poor girl, then run away before she wakes up, with no intention of calling her again.'

'How long have you been there?' Ryan said.

'Long enough,' Chloe snapped.

I picked up my tea and stood up. 'It's none of your business, Chlo.' I walked past her, through the doorway and into the hall.

I could feel Chloe bristling behind me. 'I can't believe you went that far with someone behind Eve's back. God, you are so sad.'

'SHUT UP,' I yelled, suddenly furious. 'You don't know anything about it. This hasn't got anything to do with Eve.'

Chloe stared at me. Her eyes were hard. I knew that expression well – she was itching for a fight. 'I wonder if that's how Eve'll see it,' she said nastily.

I clenched my fists. 'You're not going to tell her.' Fear

flooded through me. What would Eve say if she knew? She would understand, wouldn't she? It's not like I planned what happened. And, after all, Eve had said she didn't want me any more. I had no idea when she was coming back. *If* she was coming back.

I tried to imagine telling her. 'She mustn't know,' I said.

Chloe opened her mouth, but before she could say anything, the phone rang. She darted into the kitchen and picked it up.

'Matt? What's happening?'

A minute later she was back. 'Luke?' Her eyes filled with tears. 'They're really worried about Mum at the hospital. They've got to do an emergency caesarian – cut the baby out. Matt says we should go down there now.'

I fell asleep slumped across three hospital waiting-room chairs at about seven am. We'd arrived at the hospital just as Mum had gone into the operating theatre. Chloe went off to leave a message with work that she was going to have to miss her first day.

We'd hardly spoken on the way here in the taxi. We'd dropped Ryan off at his house – I noticed he and Chloe hadn't said goodbye to each other, but I didn't give it much thought. I was fighting hard to stay awake the whole time. I could see Chloe was worried about Mum, but I wasn't. I couldn't believe for a second anything bad could happen to her. I mean, she was only having a baby. Even if it wasn't happening the normal way. People had babies every day.

As I slept I dreamed of Eve. Not the normal X-rated dreams I had about her. But one where her face kept floating in front of me, her eyes full of hurt. *Don't you love me, Luke?* And I kept reaching out to touch her face, to tell her that I did love her. That I loved her more than anything. But she kept floating away, out of reach.

I woke up, missing her so hard it was like a stone in my chest. Chloe was shaking my shoulder.

'Mum's OK. She's had the baby. A boy. We can go in and see her.'

I stared up at her, bleary-eyed. It took me a few seconds to take in what she was saying. I sat up, blinking.

Chloe's lips trembled. 'I was so worried.' Tears leaked out of her eyes. 'Imagine if she'd died too, Luke.' She bent over, crying.

I put my arm around her, yawning. 'Hey. Hey. It's all right,' I said, rubbing my hand over her shoulder.

Chloe nestled against me. 'I'm sorry I was such a bitch earlier,' she sniffed. 'I mean, I suppose I did *tell* you to go out on a date with Hayley, and it's not your fault if she's a total slut and your brain's in your trousers.'

I grinned. Only Chloe could turn an apology into an insult in a single sentence.

'Come on,' I said. 'Let's go and see Mum.'

A nurse took us down to one of the little rooms off the main ward. Mum lay in bed, asleep. Matt was sitting beside her, his face in his hands. As we reached the bed, he looked up.

'She's resting,' he whispered. 'Don't go upsetting her.'

*For goodness sake.*

'We're not going to upset her,' I whispered back. 'We just wanted to make sure she was all right.'

'She's fine.' Matt sighed. 'It was awful, though. Worse for me, to be honest. She was totally out of it once they started drugging her up. But then they started trying to get the baby out and they couldn't and . . . anyway . . . it's all over now.'

'Where's the baby?' Chloe said.

'Baby Unit.' Matt sighed, again. 'He was premature, remember. They say he's OK – they're just making sure, I think.' He paused. 'Your mum wants to call him Sam. '

As Mum was fast asleep, Matt offered to take us up to see the baby. We had to wash our hands before going into the ward – there were rows of little cots, some of them attached to big machines. Matt took us over to a cot in the corner. A tiny bundle of blue blanket was rolled up in the

41

middle of it, a scrunched-up red face peeking out of the top.

'He's beautiful,' Chloe breathed.

I stared at the baby. 'Beautiful' was not the word I would have chosen. In fact, 'pigging ugly' would have been closer to the truth. Still . . .

'He looks like you, Matt,' I said.

Matt shrugged. 'Yeah, the nurses said that, too.'

Chloe asked if she could hold the baby and one of the nurses helped her take him in her arms. They asked me if I wanted to hold him too. I said no. He was way too scarily small and floppy.

Chloe oohed and aahed for a bit. Then we went back downstairs to see if Mum was awake. She was sitting up in bed, still looking a bit pale. She said she was going to be in hospital for a few days. She asked Chloe again not to move out – but Chloe was adamant.

'I'm sorry but I can't not, Mum. I've already had to take today off work and I'm paying rent on the flat as from right now. I gotta go in tomorrow – it's the busiest time, just before Christmas.'

Mum looked dopily over at me.

'Luke, I want you to go and stay at Matt's, then.'

I shook my head. 'No way, Mum. I'll be fine on my own. I'll call Trisha if there's any problem.'

Mum glanced at Matt.

*Don't look at him. It hasn't got anything to do with him.*

Matt shrugged. I could tell he was relieved.

Mum looked back at me. 'OK, but no parties, Luke. No . . . no mucking about.' She stared at me as if she could see exactly what I'd done last night. I blushed.

Matt gave me and Chloe a lift home. Three hours later Chloe walked out, a large bag in either hand, to take the tube down to her new place. As I watched her wandering down the road, I realised she hadn't spoken to Ryan since we got back, not even to let him know about the baby. I wondered again what exactly was going on with them.

What a weird day. Sex. A baby brother. And now I was going to spend the night in the house on my own. I'd never done that before. Whenever Mum had gone away before – and it hadn't happened very often – Chloe had always been there.

I heated up some leftover food in the fridge, then wandered from room to room. It was spookily quiet without Mum and Chloe shouting at each other.

I finished eating and left the bowl, quite deliberately, in the middle of the living-room floor. Mum always told me off for doing that. But she wasn't here to order me to pick it up. I was free to do whatever I wanted.

43

Some carol singers came to the door. I gave them fifty pence from the jar of change Mum kept in the kitchen. It was going to be Christmas next week. I wondered if Eve would send me a card.

*Don't hold your breath.*

I thought about calling Ry, seeing if he wanted to come round. But I decided against it. It felt weird being on my own – but good . . . grown up, if a little bit lonely. I wanted to make the most of it while it lasted.

I ran myself a deep, hot bath. Trisha rang while I was still in the water to ask how Mum was. Matt had apparently called her, on Mum's instructions, from the hospital.

'I'll pop round tomorrow at some point, Luke,' she said. 'Bring you some dinner.'

'Thanks,' I said, shivering in my towel.

Afterwards I watched a bit of TV, spent a deeply satisfying half-hour reliving, again, everything that had happened with Hayley, then decided to go to bed.

I was totally knackered. I'd had a total of about three hours sleep in the whole of the last day and a half.

As I lay down, my eyes fell on the picture of Eve on my bedside table. She was so beautiful. I gazed at her face, at the total sexiness of her smile. I wished she was here right now. Not to do anything – I was too tired to even think about that for once – but just to wrap my arms around.

I closed my eyes.

Her face was still in my head, imprinted against my eye-lids.

I pulled the pillow down, imagining I was holding her. *Eve*.

# 6

# Looking after Sam

Mum came home after four days, but Sam stayed in hospital for another week. Mum went back every day, spending hour after hour in the Special Baby Unit. I went with her a few times but it was phenomenally boring – and depressing too. Sam was fine, just a bit small, but some of the babies in there were really ill. There were always anxious parents padding about, often in tears.

On top of that, Mum spent most of her time in the hospital trying to breastfeed. The first time, she just whipped out her boobs while I was standing there.

'Mum,' I hissed. 'Stop.'

She looked up at me, a slightly dazed expression in her eyes. 'What're you talking about?' she said.

'You can't do that in front of all these people,' I said.

'For goodness sake, Luke, it's perfectly natural. That's what they're there for. How do you think I fed you?' She carried on unbuttoning her top.

'Mu-um.' I gritted my teeth. 'OK, then I'm going home.'
And I left.

It's all very well her saying it's natural. There's nothing natural for *me* about seeing my mum's boobs in action. *Ugh.*

Sam came home on Christmas Eve morning and Mum got all excited about us having a family Christmas together. We didn't have much food in, so she sent me down to the shops to buy some cartons of soup and nice bread.

But Christmas Day was a disaster. Firstly, the baby didn't sleep at all the night before. Worse, he cried the whole time. A horrible, mewing cry like a drowning kitten. I shut my door and shoved two pillows over my head, but his bawling still woke me up about twenty times.

Then Chloe phoned and said she couldn't make it home after all – she'd been invited to lunch with one of the girls from her new flat. Mum came off the phone crying, and she didn't really stop all day.

Matt arrived at about eleven o'clock with loads of booze. Then he and Mum had a massive argument about the fact there was no Christmas lunch.

'I can't drink, I'm breastfeeding,' she said. 'And just when did you think I'd have time to shop for a turkey dinner?' she said.

47

'You brought Sam back over twenty-four hours ago,' Matt said, staring at her blankly. 'Surely you could have made it to the supermarket.'

I wanted to hit him. Couldn't he see how exhausted Mum was?

And then Mum started apologising to him for everything being in such a mess and, frankly, I felt like hitting her.

We ate soup and beans-on-toast for lunch, after which the baby finally went to sleep. Mum crashed out about two seconds later and Matt sat around, drinking and watching TV.

I noticed he made no effort to wash up the lunch things so I did it, feeling very sorry for myself. Afterwards, as I wandered past the living-room door I heard Mum – clearly now awake – squeal with excitement.

'Oh, look, Matt. He's really latched on this time.'

I could hear Matt grunting, uninterested.

I grimaced. I knew from my hospital visits that 'latched on' was some kind of breastfeeding term. I headed for the stairs.

'I think that means he'll take a proper feed, now,' Mum was saying. 'Goodness, I never had this trouble with Chloe and Luke.'

About an hour later they had another argument. I could

hear them from my room. Mum was trying to persuade Matt to stay the night. He was explaining – entirely unconvincingly – that he had to pop in on some elderly relatives before it got too late.

'You've never bothered with them before.' Mum was sobbing. 'Oh, Matt. Please stay. I'm exhausted. I really need your help.'

She sounded so pitiful I couldn't believe it when Matt started shouting again. 'But it never lets up. We never get a break from him,' he yelled.

*We? Where were* you *last night, while Mum and I were enduring the drowning kitten hours?*

Then Mum totally lost it. She started screaming at him for being selfish and cruel and not caring about her and the baby.

I sat in my room, delighted she was finally standing up to him.

*You tell him, Mum.*

Then the front door slammed shut. Silence.

After a few minutes I crept down and peered round the living-room door. Mum was sitting in Dad's old armchair, rocking Sam in her arms. Her face was haggard and stained with tears.

'I'm sorry, baby,' she was saying. 'I'm sorry. I'm sorry.'

I stood by the door, uncertain what to do. I hate seeing

Mum cry. It makes me feel so helpless. And – if I'm honest – it's scary, too. I wanted to go up to her, but I had no idea what to say. I desperately wished Dad was here.

Or Chloe.

Or Eve.

'Mum?' I said, hesitantly.

She didn't seem to hear me. Just carried on rocking.

I did the only thing I could think of. I went into the kitchen and called Trisha.

She was brilliant. She was in the middle of some big family Christmas on the other side of town, but she came straight over with Alice, her little girl. When she arrived, she took one look at Mum, still weeping in the living room, and sent her up to bed.

'I'll look after Sam for a bit,' she said firmly. 'You need some sleep.'

Once Mum had dragged herself upstairs, Trisha smiled at my anxious face. 'Thanks for calling me, Luke. Your mum's lucky to have you. Don't worry, she'll be fine. She's just exhausted. And Matt the prat isn't helping.'

I grinned at her. I knew Trisha's baby was due soon – she had this round bump that stuck out a long way in front – but she didn't seem to have slowed down or cracked up like Mum.

Then Sam woke up and started wailing again. We went

into the kitchen so Trisha could make up a bottle of milk for him. She made me stay and watch how it was done. Then she got me to change his nappy.

'So you can give your mum a break every now and then,' she said. 'OK?'

I nodded. If anyone else had tried to give me baby-care lessons, I'd probably have told them where to shove it. But Trisha made it sound like we were equal partners trying to help Mum out. Changing the nappy wasn't so difficult, either. Alice watched me, squatting down on her heels.

Trisha looked round the kitchen. 'Now,' she said. 'I realise you've done your best to stay on top of things, but it is a bit of a mess in here.'

I looked round. 'A bit of a mess' was an understatement. Despite the fact that I had washed up the beans saucepan and the plates, there was baby stuff everywhere, plus some dirty bowls from two days ago I'd shoved in a corner – and piles and piles of clothes that needed washing.

'You take Alice to the park,' she said. 'I'm going to have a clear up.'

Alice held my hand as we went down to the park. She was a sweet little kid, really. Big shiny brown eyes like Trisha and wispy pigtails. She chattered on about her Christmas presents, telling me about the pregnant Barbie she'd been given. 'It's got a baby in its tummy and everything. Just like Mummy.'

We wandered past the small pond and I thought of Eve. This was where we'd met up for those first few days we were together. Where we'd made out in the sunshine.

'Luke.' Alice tugged on my hand. 'So what did you get?'

'What?' I tore myself away from a delicious memory of lying on the grass with Eve.

'For Christmas. What presents did *you* get?'

I realised with a jolt that I hadn't had any presents. Well, Mum had promised me some money, but hadn't actually got round to giving it to me. And Chloe had left me a scrawled IOU promising to buy me a drink when we next saw each other. But that was it. Mum's parents were dead and she was an only child. And Mum had totally fallen out with the whole of Dad's family when she'd started going out with Matt, so I'd just had a note and a (small) cheque to share with Chloe from my grandparents in Scotland.

'When you get bigger, sometimes you don't get presents,' I said.

*Or cards. Or anything from your girlfriend . . . How's your Christmas holiday going, Eve?*

I pushed Alice on the swings in the children's playground for a bit, then we wandered back home.

Mum was still asleep. So, miraculously, was Sam. And the house was sparkling.

Trisha pulled on her coat. 'I left a bottle in the fridge for Sam. If he wakes up, heat it up like I showed you and feed him. And don't take any nonsense from your Mum about how she's a terrible mother if she doesn't breastfeed every hour of the day. She's so tired . . . I'm guessing she's not eating enough to produce the milk she needs at the moment. So, make her rest and eat, and supplement with formula tonight, OK? I'll call round tomorrow and the health visitor should be popping in, too.'

I nodded, wondering how I could possibly have a conversation with Mum about breastfeeding without dying of embarrassment.

In the end it wasn't an issue. Sam woke. I fed him. It was a bit scary at first, but he sucked so hard on the bottle, his little jaws working furiously, that I decided he was probably stronger than I'd realised. He still looked kind of scrunched up and ugly though. More like an old man than my idea of a baby.

Mum seemed better when she woke up. She was nearly in tears again when she realised how much Trisha had done – and that I'd fed Sam.

'I'm so lucky to have you,' she said. 'And a good friend like Trisha.'

*As opposed to Matt the prat?*

I said nothing.

Matt put in an appearance the next day. But he didn't stay long. I noticed that he didn't offer to help feed Sam or to get him off to sleep. In fact, he didn't even seem to want to hold him. I mean, I didn't particularly want to either. But Matt was his *dad*. Mum was depressed again after he'd gone. Still, she cheered up a bit when Trisha came round.

Over the next few days I kept on helping out – changing nappies, giving Sam bottles of milk and running shopping errands for Mum. I met up with Ryan a few times. He'd had a great Christmas away at his uncle's – making out with one of his cousin's friends outside the church at some carol service on Christmas Eve.

I asked him if he missed Chloe. Apparently they hadn't spoken since she moved out a week ago. I'd tried to ring her myself a few times, basically to tell her to come home and help out, but she was avoiding my calls.

'I sort of miss her.' Ryan shrugged. 'But this is what she wanted.'

I couldn't make sense of either of them.

New Year's Eve was a bad day. Eve and I had talked about it months ago – how much we both loved the idea of being together right at the start of the year. And here we were –

miles apart. On top of which Matt demanded he and Mum go out for the evening – and then stormed out when Mum said Sam wasn't settled enough to leave with a babysitter.

Mum took Sam round to Trisha's in floods of tears again.

I trudged along to the Burger Bar at about nine. I knew Ryan would be in there with a crowd of friends. They were meeting up, then going back to someone's house for an all-nighter. I was hardly in the mood for a party, but if anyone could cheer me up, it would be Ryan.

He was slightly drunk when I arrived, his arms round two girls from my class. I didn't like that much. Despite everything he and Chloe had said, it still felt weird seeing him with other people.

'Luke, man, the party's gonna be great. And I know at least three girls who're desperate for you to be there,' he bellowed, punching me in the shoulder.

I winced. Everyone at the table was looking at me. I sat down opposite Ryan, my face burning.

'One of them isn't Hayley, is it?' I whispered as soon as everyone turned away. The last thing I wanted was to see her again.

Ryan tried to shrug and wink at the same time. 'You'll see,' he said. We stayed in the Burger Bar until about ten-thirty, then everyone started fumbling about, getting their stuff together to go to the party. Half the girls at the table made a mass trip to the bathroom.

I was seriously thinking about just going home. As I pulled my jacket from the pile on the floor, my phone fell out. Six missed calls. I didn't recognise the number.

'He's fit.' One of the girls still sitting at the table pointed towards the door. She giggled. 'Can't you ask him to come to the party, too?'

I followed the girl's pointing finger.

A tall, good-looking guy in his late teens was standing in the doorway, looking anxiously round the room. His hair was dark and swept back off his strong, square-jawed face.

'Hey.' My eyes widened. 'Look, Ry. It's Alejandro.'

Alejandro. This really sound guy we'd met in Spain in the summer. The guy I had mistakenly thought Eve had got off with one night. I hadn't seen him since the day we'd left Jonno's hotel at the end of August. He'd sent me and Ryan a couple of postcards from places where he and his band had been on tour this autumn.

'NO WAY!' Ryan's yell was deafening. He leaped to his feet and headed for the doorway.

The girls at the table were still gawping at Alejandro. 'Can you believe Ry knows him?' one of them said.

'Can't see a girlfriend, can you?'

'Piss off. I saw him first.'

56

I smiled to myself, wanting to tell them they had no chance. Alejandro was gay. I got up to go over, thinking how sorry Eve would be that she'd missed him.

And then my breath caught in my throat. I knew Alejandro's tour included lots of dates in Spain. Maybe he'd seen Eve. Maybe he knew where she was.

I scrambled past the girls at the table and pushed my way over to the door. Alejandro saw me coming. As soon as I got near enough, we both started speaking at the same time.

'What's happened?' I said. 'Why are you here?'

'Thank God I have found you,' Alejandro said. 'We called and called and drove everywhere. Eve thought you might be here.'

My heart leaped. 'Eve? Have you spoken to her? Is she all right?'

For the first time Alejandro's face relaxed.

'Better than that, man,' Ryan slurred beside him.

I stared at Alejandro, my heart now beating wildly. 'What?' I said. 'What's going on?'

Alejandro grinned at me. 'We will talk in the car. Come on.'

He turned towards the door.

I grabbed his arm. 'Where's Eve?'

'Waiting for you.' He pointed to the street. 'Out there.'

# 7

# Something in his jeans

I followed Alejandro outside the Burger Bar, Ryan beside me. My eyes were everywhere, looking for Eve.

I couldn't believe she was really here.

Alejandro stopped. He turned to Ryan.

'It is better if you go back,' he said.

Ryan screwed up his face. 'I want to see Eve too,' he said.

'No. She doesn't want anyone knowing she's here. You must go back. Stop anyone else coming out here. And don't say you've seen her.'

'What?' Ryan said. 'Why?'

Alejandro frowned.

'Because she's run away, hasn't she?' I said. The whole situation suddenly made sense. 'Her dad has no idea she's here.'

Alejandro nodded. 'But here is the first place he will look,' he said. 'Ryan, you must do this. Please. Listen to Luke.'

Ryan nodded solemnly. 'OK, man. Not a word.' He turned and slouched back to the Burger Bar.

'Come on.' Alejandro checked the heavy gold watch that hung round his wrist. 'We need to be going – we took so much time getting a hire car from the airport.'

He crossed the road and disappeared round the first street on the right. I hurried after him, my heart pounding. Round the corner, Alejandro headed towards a white Ford Mondeo. I strained to see inside. It was too dark. My hands shook as I walked towards it. Then the front passenger door opened. *Eve?* A pair of long, slim, jean-clad legs slid onto the pavement.

She stood up. My stomach twisted.

It was her. Really her. A little blue hat pulled down over her sleek, blonde hair. She was beyond beautiful. Beyond desirable.

Eve. Smiling at me.

I stopped, completely poleaxed by the shock of it. Of how she looked. Of how I felt.

We stared at each other. My feet were stuck to the pavement, like I'd fall down if I took a single step.

She was standing right in front of me. That perfect, heart-shaped face. Those pale blue eyes, glistening in the light from the street lamps, pulling me in. My heart raced as we leaned towards each other, our faces moving closer, almost touching, the whole world shrinking to the feel of her breath on my skin.

I wound my arms round her. She was real. Warm. Clinging on to me, crying. I held her as tight as I could, feeling the curves of her body against mine. Her tears on my cheek.

'It's all right now. It's . . .' I whispered.

But she was twisting round, searching for my mouth.

The kiss exploded in my head. I forgot where I was. I forgot even that I was standing up.

Eve didn't stop kissing me. And I couldn't let go of her.

Eventually I registered that Alejandro was hopping up and down beside us, talking.

'Listen. Luke. Eva. We have to go now. It is almost eleven.'

I drew back a little, but I couldn't look away from her. Out of the corner of my eye I could see Alejandro gesticulating wildly with his hands. 'Get in the car.' He ushered us towards the back seat. '*Hijo de* . . . God. You two. And please do not take your clothes off.'

I grinned at Eve, then let her go. She slid across the back seat, then looked back, reaching out for me as I got in. We started making out again, our arms wrapped round each other.

I could hear Alejandro getting into the front seat and starting the engine. My eyes were wide open, soaking in Eve's blissed-out face as she kissed me.

She looked up at me, arching her eyebrows. 'Your heart's beating fast,' she whispered.

'Oh yeah?' I said quietly. 'My hands are cold, too.'

I reached under her jumper and pressed my palms against her waist, feeling her flinch from the cold. I pressed harder, grinning, not letting her wriggle away. She smiled at me, moving closer, stroking my face with her fingers.

I wanted her so badly, I was almost paralysed with it. As my hands warmed up, I slid them round her back, running them up and down her bare skin. My hands were as hot as the rest of me now, but I could still feel her shivering under my fingers.

How horny was that?

'Now whose heart's beating fast?' I murmured.

I brought my hands round to her front. She stared up at me, her breathing all ragged.

So I ripped off her clothes and . . .

Only joking. Unfortunately. What actually happened was that she glanced over at Alejandro in the front seat and pushed my hands away.

I nodded, reluctantly, to show I understood. Eve had never liked touching and stuff in front of other people.

*OK. I can wait. I think.*

I put my arm round her shoulders.

'Tell me what happened,' I said. 'Tell me everything.'

Eve explained quickly how the convent school operated. It sounded like something out of the nineteenth century – all old-fashioned customs and strict discipline.

'At first all I thought about was running away, getting back to you.' Eve snuggled right up against me and laid her head on my chest. 'It's so awful there, Luke. I mean, some of the nuns are OK and the other girls are all right – but they're all Spanish. A few speak quite good English, but there isn't anyone I can talk to properly.'

'So did you try?' I said. 'Running away, I mean?'

Eve nodded. 'But the convent was in the middle of nowhere. I had no idea where I was, just that it was miles from the nearest town. The nuns thought the internet was the work of *El Diablo* – the devil – so, no email.' She rolled her eyes. 'I mean, for God's sake. There was, like, one phone, practically guarded with dogs. And the post got taken out once a week – I tried to write to you, but my dad left instructions they were to check all my mail. It was like being in a prison camp.'

I kissed her head, taking in a long, deep breath of her apple-smelling hair. Outside the car, roads I didn't recognise were flashing by.

'Tell him about Christmas,' Alejandro said.

'OK.' Eve twisted her soft, slender fingers through mine. 'After I'd been there, kicking against it all, for about two months – begging Mum to get me out – Dad started talking about me staying the whole year and I realised two things. If I was going to get away I'd have to make it happen myself. And I had to start acting like I was changing, so Dad would start trusting me a bit and let me come out of the school for Christmas. So I made that call to my mum – which he was listening to – saying I wanted you to forget all about me.' She reached up and grazed my ear. 'Which I didn't mean at all,' she whispered, her voice all low and raspy. 'I missed you so much. I was so worried you'd just forget all about me.'

I squeezed her arm, massively turned on by her breath against my ear. 'No chance,' I murmured, kissing my way across her cheek.

'*Mierda*! Guys!' Alejandro glanced over his shoulder. 'Christmas. Eva. *Por dios.*'

Eve sat back, smiling. 'OK. Christmas. At first I thought Dad was going to leave me in the convent over the holidays. So I worked on him and worked on him. And in the end he agreed to let me come back to the hotel for a few days. But even there he made it really hard for me to talk to anyone or make calls, and I know he had that slag he's sleeping with now – the head receptionist, remember? – he had her make sure all the staff were spying on me. But he'd told me Alejandro was coming round with his dad for this big meal on Boxing Day. So . . .'

'So I arrived and there was Eva and she asked me to rescue her.' Alejandro looked at me in the rear-view mirror.

'Why didn't you call me?' I gazed past Eve, out of the side window. We were speeding along a motorway now, distant houses rushing past.

Eve sighed. 'I was worried you'd do something stupid like try and fly out to Mallorca. And I didn't want Dad to have any idea what I was planning.'

'Which was . . .?' I said. I was struggling slightly with the feeling that it should have been me, not Alejandro, helping Eve.

Eve seemed to sense what I was thinking. She took my hand. 'You don't know how paranoid I felt. I couldn't be sure Dad hadn't bugged the phone. I really wouldn't put it past him.' Her voice shook. 'And I knew that Alejandro had the money to get me out of the country. What could you have done from here?'

'I know,' I said, curling her fingers up in my hand.

'So . . . I was supposed to play a gig on New Year's Eve in Madrid,' Alejandro said. 'But I drove to La Bonita that morning . . . this morning.'

'And, by then, I think Dad was really starting to believe I'd come round to staying at the convent school,' Eve said.

'So I waited till he was in a meeting, then got my passport out of his office.'

'And I smuggled her out to the airport, bought her a ticket and here we are,' Alejandro added.

'But you came too,' I said. 'You blew out your gig tonight?'

Alejandro shrugged. 'What else could I do? I could no leave Eva on her own. Where was she going to go once she was here?'

'You could have come to me,' I said.

'Your house is the first place my dad's going to look for me,' Eve said.

I frowned, the difficulty of the situation hitting me properly for the first time. 'So, where are you . . . we . . . going?' I said.

'I have a friend. George. A musician. He lives in Cornwall,' Alejandro said.

'Cornwall?' I said. 'But that's miles away.'

'It's just for a while, Luke,' Eve said, stroking my arm.

'But then what?' I said.

Eve shook her head. 'I don't know,' she said. 'But I can't go back to my mum. She'll just do what my dad tells her. And I'm never going back to that school.'

I stared at her. 'But . . . how? I mean . . . what . . .?'

'God, Luke. *I don't know.* I just know both my parents

have let me down so badly that I . . . that I'm not sure I care if I ever see either of them again.' Tears welled up in her eyes.

I hugged her, feeling deeply troubled.

'Does your mum know where you are?' I said.

Eve shook her head. 'I called her from the airport to tell her not to worry. That I'd get in touch when I could.' She wiped her eyes. 'Hey,' she said, forcing a smile. 'How's *your* mum? Has she had the baby?'

I told her about Sam, impressing her with my nappy-changing and bottle-making abilities. Then I had a bit of a vent about how useless Matt was and then I filled her in about Ryan and Chloe.

By the time I'd finished answering all Eve's questions it was nearly one am.

'Hey, we missed Happy New Year,' Alejandro said.

'I didn't.' Eve grinned. 'I'm having it. Right now.'

I called and left a message for Mum at home, saying I was spending the night at Ryan's and probably wouldn't be back until late tomorrow. Then I called Ry to get him to cover for me. I had no intention of going home tomorrow, of course, but I decided I'd deal with one day at a time. Like Eve.

'You know we will have to stop for the night.' Alejandro yawned. 'I can't drive for much longer. I was up really early to drive to La Bonita this morning.'

There were a number of hotels listed on the map Alejandro had bought from the car-hire company, but it took a while to find one with spare rooms. Everywhere was full of New Year's Eve partygoers. By the time we found a place – a motel off the motorway in Somerset that the car hire guy had recommended – it was nearly two am. Eve had started yawning as much as Alejandro.

'I didn't sleep much last night either,' she told me. 'I was too excited.'

I was so focused on getting her alone, that I actually opened my mouth to tell her not to plan on sleeping too much tonight either. Then it suddenly struck me that she might be assuming I'd share with Alejandro. After all, we had never spent the whole night on our own together before.

The double horror of this – not being with Eve while having to share a room with someone gay – filled my head as I watched Alejandro pay cash for two rooms. I was sure he and Eve hadn't discussed the sleeping arrangements in the car. Maybe they'd talked about it earlier.

As we trudged upstairs I tried – and failed – to catch Eve's eye.

Alejandro, clearly dead on his feet from tiredness, stopped halfway along the corridor. He muttered goodnight and stumbled inside the room to his left. The door shut behind him.

*Yes.* I slipped my arm round Eve's waist as we walked a bit further along to our room.

*Our room.*

'Can I share your toothbrush?' I whispered as Eve turned the key and opened the door.

She smiled sexily at me. 'You can share everything,' she said.

The room was small and girly-pretty, dominated by the big, flowery-quilted bed against the far wall. Fluttery pink curtains were drawn open at the window. Eve went across and looked out, into the dark countryside around the hotel.

She shrugged off her jacket and raked back her hair, unaware of how intently I was watching her.

There was something different about her. I'd sensed it earlier, without realising it properly. Now, seeing her move around, it was obvious. Eve'd always had this deep-down sexiness, this natural way of moving like a cat. But now she seemed more sure of herself too. More confident.

She drew the curtains and turned around to face me. Her cheeks were a little pink. 'Luke,' she said slowly. 'I've been thinking . . .'

'What?'

She was so beautiful. So sexy. I couldn't believe she was real. And here. With me. All night.

'Before, I thought it might be weird seeing you after such a long time. I thought it might feel awkward. But it just felt right. Really natural. Didn't it?'

I nodded. There was a long pause.

'Anyway, I was thinking about how it used to be, before, with us, and I . . . I've realised I've changed.'

I stood rooted to the spot. What was she talking about? How had she changed?

'I don't understand,' I said.

Eve smiled. 'I used to worry about what other people would think of me and . . . and I guess it just felt wrong but now . . . now it's different. Before, I didn't really want to. Now, I can't see how I can stop myself. Or why I should. D'you see?'

I shook my head, fear threading like a worm through my head. 'Eve, I have no idea what you're talking about.'

She took a deep breath. 'I'm just saying that I want to . . . I want to . . . you know . . . with you,' she said. 'I'm ready.'

My heart seemed to stop.

'That is, if you want to,' she grinned.

I stared at her, in total shock. Sex – full sex – had always been this kind of forbidden topic between us. Eve's six months older than me and, when we met, her boyfriend Ben was pushing her to do it with him. At first I was just desperate to get her away from him, so I was always careful not to be pushy myself. Then, later, when I got all jealous over other guys lusting after her, I was too scared of her going off me to even talk to her about actually doing it. It was only in the last few days of our holiday that we'd come close. Really close, sometimes. But even so, she made it clear it wasn't an option. I mean, maybe if we'd had more time . . .

'You do *want* to, don't you?' Eve was now frowning at me.

A massive smile spread across my face. 'God, yes. *Yes.*'

Eve smiled gently back, reaching out to hold my hands. 'I thought about it a lot when I was in Spain. Losing my virginity is a really, really big deal to me. But then, so are you.'

I started kissing her, my heart racing.

'Wait.' Eve wriggled away from me and pulled off her trainers. She sat down on the bed. 'There's something I've got to ask you.'

'What?' I lay down beside her and ran my finger down her face.

*Please let it be a quick something . . .*

Eve bit her lip. 'I just want to know if you went out

70

with anyone while I was in Spain. I mean, I'd understand if you did, so you can be honest. I thought about that a lot too and though I hated the idea, I knew that I couldn't blame you if you went on a date or something. Or even if you ended up kissing someone one evening.' She looked away from me, at the flowery quilt on the bed. 'I mean, I know after what I told Mum you must've thought I'd be away for a whole year . . . and I couldn't expect you to stay in every night. And . . . well . . .' She tailed off miserably.

My stomach twisted into a knot. I rolled away from her and lay back on the bed, staring up at the ceiling. There was no way I could tell her about Hayley. Not after her saying all that about how losing her virginity was such a big deal. If she sounded miserable at the thought of a date or a kiss . . .

No. I couldn't say anything. It would really hurt her.

*Not to mention drastically reduce the chances of us actually getting to have sex.*

But how was I going to lie to her?

As Ryan had once put it, I was the world's worst liar.

Eve's face appeared above me. 'OK, you're scaring me, Luke. How many girls did you go out with?'

I stared up at her.

*Be honest. Be absolutely, literally, honest.*

'None,' I said. 'Not one. I didn't chat up a single girl. I didn't ask a single girl out. I didn't even see anyone who I wanted to talk to. Well, maybe I talked to a few – but only because Ryan forced me to.' I stopped before I ran off track into a lie. I cupped Eve's face in my hands. 'I thought about you all the time,' I said. 'I missed you every single day.'

That *was* the truth and I could see her believing it, her pale blue eyes soft in the low light seeping in from the corridor outside the room.

We kissed. A long, agonisingly sexy kiss. I was only focused on where she'd said we were going. On what she'd said we could do. I wanted it so much it was almost unbearable. My hands ran down her jumper then tugged at her jeans, fumbling with the button.

But Eve just sighed and turned round, snuggling backwards into my arms. 'Luke?' she murmured.

'Yes?' I said, softly, reaching down with my hands again.

She yawned. 'I feel so safe with you.'

I blinked, confused by this change of tack. 'What?' I said.

I could feel Eve's whole body shudder as she yawned again. 'I'm so tired now that . . . that . . .' She reached out for my hand and pulled my arm right across her, like I was a blanket, tucking her in. 'This feels like home,' she murmured sleepily.

My arm was now resting tantalisingly under her chest. I hugged her, gently trying to pull my hand free. Then I felt her relax – her hand releasing mine, her whole body softening back into me and onto the mattress.

'Eve?' I whispered.

*Please don't fall asleep.*

'Eve?' I peered round at her face. Too late. Her eyes were closed and her breathing was soft and even.

I groaned out loud. *Don't do this to me, Eve.*

But she just lay there on top of the flowery quilt.

The frustration driving through me was like nothing I'd ever felt before. I wanted to thump something. Gritting my teeth I turned away and pounded at the pillow, then I sank down and stared longingly at Eve's slender body. I could hear her breath getting deeper, taking her further and further away from me.

I think if it had been any other girl in the world I would have tried to shake her awake. Quite hard probably. But Eve looked so vulnerable – all curled up on the bed. I was seized by this fierce need to look after her. To protect her from anything bad that might happen.

I wrapped my arms back around her and buried my face in her hair.

*Nothing and no one are taking you away again. Ever.*

# 8
# Running away

I couldn't work out what the noise was. Some kind of banging or thumping. Like a hammer on a plank of wood. It was dragging me up from a deep sleep, forcing me to notice it. Forcing me to wake up.

Where was I? I was dimly aware I was lying down, holding something. Some*one*. Eve. The memory of her, of everything that had happened flooded through me.

The thudding sound was louder now, but I wasn't focusing on it at all. For a few semi-conscious seconds I lay there, wrapped round her, enjoying the sensation of not being able to work out where I ended, where she began.

And then I realised that the noise wasn't going away. That someone was outside, banging on the door.

'Luke. Eva. Get up.' It was Alejandro. There was something desperate about his voice.

Eve stirred slightly, moving against me.

The thumping on the door started again.

Reluctantly I disentangled my arms from hers and staggered out of bed and across the room. It was still dark outside.

I pulled open the door. Alejandro was standing there, a look of total terror on his face, his bag in his hand.

'Jonno,' he hissed. 'Here. Now. Downstairs. Come on.'

I stared at him, suddenly wide awake.

'Here?' I gasped.

*Eve's father's here?*

Alejandro gritted his teeth, barging past me into the room. He raced over to Eve on the bed and shook her roughly. 'Get up.' He picked up her trainers from the floor. 'We can get out down the fire escape.'

Eve blinked sleepily up at him. 'What?'

'Your dad,' I said, tugging on my jeans. 'He's here.'

Eve sat bolt upright, her eyes wide. 'No. How . . .?'

I shoved her sweater into her arms. 'Come on.'

As I turned round I met Alejandro's eyes. 'He'll kill us,' I said.

'*Yo se.*' Alejandro opened the door. 'I know.'

'Oh Luke.' Eve scrambled into her jumper, then raced across the room and picked up her bag.

'Eve,' I said. 'Hurry up.'

'I need this,' she said, clutching the bag.

'Let's go.' Alejandro whispered.

Holding my shoes in one hand and our jackets in the other, I followed him out onto the corridor. Eve crept beside me.

The unmistakable sound of Jonno's voice roared up from the lobby downstairs. 'I don't care how early it is. She's my bloody daughter. I know they're here – the man at the car-hire place told me he recommended you. For goodness sake, I can see the sodding hire car outside.'

'Oh, God,' Eve whimpered.

I grabbed her wrist and pulled her down the corridor towards Alejandro and the fire escape. I glanced at her as Alejandro pushed open the fire door. *Jesus*. Her whole body was shaking.

I had time to feel a stab of pure hatred for Jonno before the door scraped loudly open and we were running down the iron steps outside.

*How dare he terrorise her like this?*

It was freezing outside and still completely dark. My breath misted in the air. The steps and the dark, tarmac ground were icy cold under my bare feet.

We were at the side of the building. The hire car was in the car park at the front. To reach it we just had to run round an ivy-clad brick wall. Eve pulled her arm out of my grip as we raced along. I looked over my shoulder. She was standing still, rummaging for something in her bag.

She took out her pencil case, then hoisted her bag back on her shoulder.

'Eve,' I ran back, grabbing her arm again. 'What the hell are you *doing*?'

Alejandro had reached the wall. He peered round it, then beckoned us forwards.

I ran, heart racing, dragging Eve behind me. She was now fumbling in her pencil case. I could hear her pulling things out and them dropping on the ground. I glanced round as we reached the wall. A trail of paintbrushes and pencils led from Eve back to the fire escape. What the hell was she doing?

Eve removed something small and silvery from the case.

'They can see the hire car from the reception,' Alejandro whispered. 'We have to run.'

I looked across to the car park. All the cars were parked neatly apart from a large blue Mercedes which had been left at an angle in front of the hotel's main entrance.

It was obviously the car Jonno had just arrived in.

Alejandro's hired white Ford Mondeo was only three parking spaces away from it. I gulped, turning back to Eve.

'Ready?'

She nodded.

'Now.'

We raced across the car park. As we passed the

Mercedes I felt Eve wrench her arm away from me again. I turned round. She was bending down, jabbing the silvery thing from her bag at the car tyre.

'What the . . . ?'

I bent down, trying to pull her away. Then I realised what she was doing.

The silvery object was some sort of art knife. She'd used one like it all the time when she was working on her GCSE coursework last year. She was jabbing it against the tyre, but her hands were shaking so much it kept glancing off the rubber.

'It won't go in,' she said, desperately.

I put my hand on hers. 'Give it to me.'

She released the knife into my hand. I drew back and stabbed it with all my strength into the tyre.

I could hear Alejandro opening the door of our hire car a few metres away.

'Go and get in the car,' I whispered.

'EVE!'

Jonno's yell echoed towards us from inside the hotel.

Eve turned and vanished.

I stabbed at the tyre again, making the hole bigger.

*Yes.*

Air hissed out.

I sprang to my feet and ran to the hired car. Alejandro

was revving the engine. Reversing out of the parking space.

'EVE!'

Jonno sounded so close. I couldn't help but look round. He was there, right by the entrance to the hotel. His broad frame looked bigger than I remembered as he rushed towards me, his face twisted with fury.

I yanked open the back door of the moving car and hurled myself into the back seat. I slammed the door shut as Alejandro screeched away down the gravel drive.

Eve was curled up in a ball on the seat beside me, her hands over her ears.

I turned round just in time to see Jonno thumping the bonnet of the blue Mercedes.

'Is he coming?' Alejandro asked nervously as we pulled onto the road.

'No,' I gasped. 'But I bet he makes the hotel let him use their car or . . .'

'. . . or calls the police,' Alejandro said, grimly. '*Hijo de puta.*' He slammed his hands onto the steering wheel and pressed his foot down on the accelerator. The car zoomed even faster down the narrow country road. I checked the dashboard. We were driving at seventy miles an hour and the speedometer was rising.

'We have to dump the car,' I said. 'Alejandro. Where can we leave it that won't get you into trouble?'

I glanced anxiously out of the rear window again. There was still no sign of Jonno.

'There's another car-hire place in Taunton,' Alejandro said as we swung onto the virtually empty motorway. 'I used it before, with my dad. We can leave this car. Get a new one. Get to George's house as fast as we can.'

He slowed down slightly from the ninety miles an hour we'd been travelling at. His shoulders relaxed.

I glanced at Eve. She was still curled up in a little ball. I reached across and put my arm round her, scooping her up against my side. She was shaking uncontrollably, her hands over her face.

'Hey,' I said. 'Hey. Great idea with the knife. It worked too.'

'I'm so sorry,' she sobbed. 'I'm so sorry you two are in the middle of this.'

'Shhh.' I hugged her harder. 'It's not your fault.'

'No.' Alejandro twisted round, grinning. 'No your fault your father is a total MANIAC.'

Even Eve managed a weak laugh at that. I rubbed her arm and squeezed her to me, gradually feeling the shaking subside.

'It's all right,' I kept saying. 'It's gonna be all right.'

But in my heart I couldn't see how it could possibly be all right. Where was Eve going to go? What was she going to do? She could hardly stay with Alejandro's friend for ever. And what was she going to do for money?

I didn't even want to think about what was going to happen when ... *if* ... Jonno finally caught up with us. With me.

The sky was starting to lighten as we reached Taunton. Alejandro found a place to leave the Ford Mondeo. Then we walked over to a different car hire company and hired a green Volvo. Alejandro bribed the desk clerk not to tell anyone we'd been there.

We set off again for Cornwall, stopping only for a few minutes at a motorway café. I bought some toast and coffee for us all and Alejandro and I leaned against the car, eating, while Eve went inside to use the bathroom.

'This is no a good situation,' Alejandro said to me in a low voice. 'I was thinking the police would be after us. But now I realise they won't. Eva is sixteen, nearly seventeen. Her life is no in danger. She has called her mother and said she is OK. The police will no bother with her.'

'But that's good, isn't it?' I said. 'That means we've only got Jonno to worry about.'

Alejandro made a face. 'Exactly. Maybe if the other

authorities are involved, Jonno will be made to see he is stupid. Doing a bad thing for Eva. But this way . . .' He sighed. 'Eva will no go home to her mother now. She is alone.'

'No she isn't,' I said. 'I'm with her.'

'For how long?' Alejandro glanced sideways at me. 'I know you like her. But you are only sixteen. You are at school. You have a life. A family. There is your mother and the little baby. Can you give all that up? All that security? Just for Eva?'

I stared at him. 'Yes,' I said. 'I'd do anything for her.'

Alejandro shook his head. 'Is that you talking or your head full of sex?'

We watched Eve walking towards us.

'Just please be careful,' Alejandro said. 'For her. For yourself.'

He strolled away, into the service station, as Eve came up.

'D'you want some toast and coffee?' I said, offering her a polystyrene cup.

Eve shook her head. She leaned against me.

'Aren't you hungry?' I said, kissing the top of her head.

'No.' She paused. 'I'm only scared.'

I put my coffee cup down on the roof of the car and held her.

'Everything's going to be all right,' I said. 'I'm here. And I'm not leaving. We're together. We'll make it work.'

I stared into her beautiful, almond-shaped eyes.

I'd said it now. I'd said I'd stay with her.

'Thank you,' she breathed. 'Oh Luke, I'm so scared I feel sick.'

She hugged me tighter. *Oh God.* I was getting turned on by the feel of her body pressed against mine. In fact, I badly wanted to get right back to where we were last night.

A little groan escaped out of my mouth.

She looked up at me, her eyebrows raised.

I grinned. 'They say that making love is a cure for fear,' I said.

'What?' Eve glanced over at Alejandro, emerging from the service station. 'But, we can't . . .'

'I know,' I said, quickly, trying not to look as totally sexed-up as I felt. 'I can wait.'

*A bit. Please? Only a bit longer.*

Alejandro came back and we got into the car again. Eve seemed slightly happier than she had earlier. She even ate some toast.

But I felt more troubled than before. What Alejandro had said kept running through my mind. Was I really prepared for everything that staying with Eve might bring?

I mean, on the one hand, of course I was. I loved Eve. I

would do anything for her. And she had no one else. I wasn't even worried about the practical things – things that maybe should have bothered me far more. Money, for instance. And how we were going to find jobs. And somewhere to live. At the time I was sure we could do all that.

But Alejandro had been right. It *was* a massive thing to say I'd give up everything for her.

For a start there was school. Well, OK. I didn't care about that.

Then there were my friends. But, I reasoned, Eve and I could make new friends wherever we went. Just like we could buy whatever stuff we needed, once we had some work.

And then there was Mum. I chewed on my lip, feeling guilty. She was having such a bad time, coping with Sam. And Chloe had only just gone. Still. That wasn't my fault. And, OK, so Matt was an idiot. But Mum had friends. Well, she had Trisha, who was a brilliant friend. Mum would be all right, wouldn't she? It wasn't as if I wouldn't let her know I was OK. At that thought I dug into my pocket and checked I'd turned my phone off last night. Mum was likely to call me soon, to try and find out when I was coming home. Or else Ryan would call, wanting to know what was happening. I wondered if Jonno had spoken to either of them; what they might have said.

How long would it be before Jonno tried to call *me*? Maybe he already had. Maybe he was trying right now.

I didn't want to speak to any of them.

I glanced down at Eve. She was huddled up beside me again – all fragile with her gorgeous lips and her tight jumper and her amazing legs and . . . *Jesus.*

Alejandro had been right about that too. My head was full of sex. It was impossible to see anything clearly other than how much I wanted Eve. I couldn't disentangle the love from the sex thing – or, if I was honest, either of those feelings from how much of an ego boost it was to know that it was *me* she'd chosen to run away with.

Eve fell asleep again, her head lolling against my shoulder. I turned away, trying not to think about it all, staring out of the window as the frosted browns of the Devon fields turned into wilder, rockier Cornwall.

# 9

# Cornwall

We arrived at George's place at about nine that morning. He lived in his parents' house – a massive, jumbled pile of worn stone and dark turrets – on a cliff top in the middle of nowhere.

'No one will find you here,' Alejandro had said. 'And George's parents are away all winter.'

I stared out at the bleak landscape that led away from the house. Beyond the edge of the cliff, the sea raged. Dark waves, tipped with white foam, crashed against the rocks below.

'Is he here on his own?' I said.

Alejandro ran his hands self-consciously through his hair. 'I doubt it. But he knows we are coming. Though no this early.'

As Alejandro rang on the doorbell, I remembered. It was New Year's Day. Most people didn't get up early after New Year's Eve. Last year I hadn't got up until twelve.

But everything was different then. I hadn't met Eve. And Dad was still alive. Just. He was in the hospice. We'd gone and visited him that afternoon. He'd been too weak to speak. Suddenly I missed him desperately. Dad would have known what to do about Jonno. He would have understood the position I was in. Better than Mum, I suspected.

But he wasn't here.

No one was answering the door. The wind whipped round the side of the house, salty and freezing – straight off the sea. Eve hugged her jacket round her shoulders and leaned against me.

Alejandro rang the doorbell a second time.

After a few minutes the door creaked open. A bleary-eyed guy, about the same age as Alejandro – eighteen or so with dark, shoulder-length hair – shielded his face from the gloomy morning light.

'Bloody hell, Al,' the boy croaked in an extremely posh voice. ''s frigging middle of the night. We only went to bed about five minutes ago.'

Alejandro rolled his eyes. 'We have had a crap night, George. And a crap drive. But sorry for disturbing your beauty sleep.' He marched inside.

George stepped back unsteadily, as Eve and I followed Alejandro into a dark, wood-panelled hall. It was like some kind of castle – all wood floors and walls, with ancient oil paintings dotted along the corridor.

Eve's eyes fixed on the artwork as George led us down the corridor towards a large, surprisingly modern, steel kitchen. All the surfaces were covered. Pizza slices lay slumped over takeaway boxes, while bags of crisps and half-eaten sausage rolls were dotted among the army of empty cans, bottles and glasses. George leaned on the counter, picked up an open bottle of white wine by the sink and took a swig.

'*Ugh*.' He turned round. 'Warm and sweet. Disgusting. Still, we didn't care at four this morning.'

He grinned and his face lit up. His eyes were a startling green, almost the same colour as his grubby T-shirt, and he had dark stubble all over his chin. Something about him reminded me of Ryan.

He glanced at Eve.

'So these are your refugees, Al?' he said, raising his eyebrows. 'At least they're raising the hottie quotient.'

I moved closer to Eve, slipping my arm round her shoulders.

But George didn't notice. He was staring at Alejandro. 'So are you,' he said. 'In fact you're looking really fit.'

I froze with embarrassment as George reached over and kissed Alejandro on the lips.

*Oh my God.*

Why hadn't it occurred to me Alejandro's friend might be gay too?

I looked away, knowing my face was bright red.

I heard George laugh. 'I know what you're going to ask. He's not here – so no competition for the drums. But Cal's here. And Jess, of course.' He rolled his eyes. 'And Clara and Em and Frank and James and God knows who else. Most of them'll be gone later. Then we can jam. Yeah?'

'Sure.' Alejandro smiled. 'But I have to return to Madrid in a few days. I already missed one gig. I can't miss another. Listen, George. This is Eva. And this Luke.'

I looked up at George, hoping my face was no longer so red.

He smiled at me, his brows slightly raised – as if he were searching for the answer to a question.

I suddenly realised what the question probably was and tightened my grip on Eve's shoulder. 'Hi.' I held up my hand, palm up in a 'stop sign' gesture, to make it quite clear kissing me was in no way an option.

'Hi,' George said. He seemed to wake up properly. 'You guys want something to eat or drink. Or d'you need to crash?'

I gazed hopefully at Eve.

'I'd love a cup of tea,' she said.

*Of course.*

*Making it with your boyfriend. Or tea.*

*No contest.*

'No problemo.' George slouched over to the kettle and switched it on.

We sat in the kitchen for an hour or so. Alejandro and George did most of the talking – reminiscing and chatting about various people. The drummer in George's band – abroad at the moment – was an old mutual friend of theirs. He'd introduced Alejandro to George at some concert a couple of years ago. But whereas Alejandro was already doing loads of professional work, George's band were still trying to get decent gigs.

'Your father will help though, no?' Alejandro said.

He'd already told me George's dad was a record producer and had loads of contacts in the music business.

'Yeah, sure,' George shrugged. 'But it's not a free pass. Mum and Dad want me to go to uni first.' He grimaced in my direction. 'This is supposed to be my gap year. They think I'm working until spring, but I jacked in my job as soon as they left for Australia.' He grinned. 'We just hang out here. Cal and I play all the time. 'S great. I mean I'd rather be in London but the flat there's tiny and it isn't soundproofed so . . .'

I asked a few questions as they talked – genuinely interested in the music they were into – and also keen to remind them I was there in case they suddenly forgot and started holding hands or something.

But Eve withdrew more and more, shrinking silently away from the group, lost in her own thoughts.

George glanced at her several times. She didn't seem to notice. In fact, she only ever looked up from the table to sip at her mug of tea. George asked her a couple of questions. Eve just gave short, shy answers and withdrew again.

I could see Alejandro was as worried about her as I was. Eve had never been exactly outgoing. But I don't think either of us had ever seen her this overwhelmed and scared before.

After a while George showed us round the downstairs part of the house. It was enormous and full of twisty little corridors and oddly-shaped rooms. George said the original part of it dated from the eighteenth century. 'But we tend to hang out mostly at the front,' he said walking us through the kitchen again and out into a massive living room. It was, like the rest of the house, wood-panelled, with long, high windows, embroidered rugs on the wooden floor and lots of little tables covered with ornaments. Bottles and cans and overflowing ashtrays lay everywhere, along with an array of dirty plates and bowls. 'Bit of a mess,' George murmured. 'Cleaner comes tomorrow.'

Through an open door I could see another room with no windows and hardly any furniture. A piano stood to one side. Five or six electric guitars were propped against three large amplifiers.

Alejandro and George started discussing the merits of the drum kit which stood in the corner.

'You OK?' I whispered to Eve. 'Shall I ask if there's a room we can have or something?'

She gazed at me. 'I'd like a bit of time on my own, actually,' she said. 'I think I'll go outside for a while. D'you mind?'

'Course not,' I lied.

Eve slipped away and I sank down on one of the sofas. *She's having a hard time. Be patient.*

George and Alejandro were talking very animatedly now. Then George turned round.

'Where'd she go?' he said, his eyes wide.

I shrugged. 'Wanted some space.'

'Man, for one second I thought she'd just vanished,' George said. 'She's like an elf or a sprite or something.'

'No she's not,' I said, irritated.

'Too much sweet wine, George,' Alejandro said quickly. 'Hey. I am very tired. Show me where I am sleeping.'

We followed George to the first floor. I wasn't sure if we'd come this way before or not. George led us along another bewildering series of corridors until we came to two doors opposite each other. George pushed one open – revealing a large room complete with wooden four-poster bed and an ornate chest-of-drawers. A sink stood in one corner. The room was as big as my and Chloe's rooms put together at home.

'Bit basic, but d'you want this?' he said to me. 'Sheets and stuff are in the drawers.'

I nodded eagerly and wandered inside.

I could hear George ushering Alejandro into the room opposite. I shut the door and walked over to the window. It looked out over the side of the house. Trees. A patch of lawn and a corner of sea in the distance.

Eve was sitting on the grass, bent over something, her bag beside her.

I went over to the bed and switched on my mobile. Four missed calls from Mum, a text from Ryan demanding an update on what was happening – CALL ME U ****ER – and ten calls from another number I didn't recognise, but which I guessed must be Jonno's.

*Oh, crap.*

Then the phone rang. I stared at the name flashing up at me.

Chloe.

'Hi,' I said.

'Where the pigging hell are you?' she snapped.

'Happy New Year to you too,' I said. 'I suppose you've spoken to Ryan then?'

'Don't get arsey with me.' Her voice rose. 'D'you have any idea what you're doing to Mum?'

'What d'you mean?'

'Eve's dad's been calling and yelling at her since early this morning. She's had to leave the phone off the hook. He's threatening to kill you or get you sent to prison or God knows what. He's been on at Ry, too. Demanding to know where Eve is. Course Ry swore blind he hadn't seen either of you. But he told me about Alejandro turning up. You've got to come home, Luke. Mum's off her head worrying about—'

'Well, she shouldn't be,' I interrupted. 'I texted Mum last night. I told her I was all right—'

'Are you listening to me. Jonno's saying—'

'He's an idiot. He—'

'For Christ's sake Luke,' Chloe shouted. 'Mum's been on the phone to me for the last hour. She's—'

'So *that's* what's really bothering you! Why don't *you* go home then?'

'I've got a job and responsibilities. You're just—'

'I'm doing it for Eve.'

I switched off the phone and hurled it onto the bed beside me.

*Bloody hell.*

Now I felt guilty in about six different directions. The last thing I wanted was Mum worrying about me. Still, at least knowing Jonno had been on the phone to her made it easier to decide what I should do. If I wasn't at home and Mum didn't know where I was, there'd be no reason for Jonno to keep calling.

My jaw clenched at the thought of him shouting at her. I paced over to the window and kicked at the wall. My shoe made a tiny dent in the plaster. Dust trickled onto the floor.

Eve was still out on the grass.

I wrestled with my conscience for about two minutes. She'd said she wanted to be on her own for a bit. And yet, she'd want to know what Chloe had said. She'd want to know about her dad.

It took me nearly ten minutes to find my way downstairs and out of the house. It was nearly ten am now, and there was no sign of anyone else about. Outside the sun had burned through the clouds and was shining on the sea, making the water glitter like broken glass. The wind was still fierce though, whipping over the cliff top and biting at my face.

I was in a really black mood as I walked towards Eve.

She heard me coming and twisted round.

'D'you mind me being here?' I said, stopping a metre or so away from her.

She shook her head. 'I'm just drawing,' she said. She gave me this sad smile that made me feel mean for being so annoyed.

'Can I see?'

She nodded.

I walked up to her and sat down, putting my arms around her. Her hands were ice cold.

'Hey, you're freezing.' I smiled at her, holding both of her hands in one of mine to warm them up.

Just being near her made me feel better. I could feel my bad mood slipping away. A seagull squawked overhead as I kissed her neck and looked down at the sketch book in her lap. It was open at a page showing a pencil drawing of the cliff top with the trees and sea beyond. It was obviously unfinished, but clearly a picture of the scene in front of us.

'That's amazing,' I said, impressed. I leaned over and flicked through the sketch pad. It was crammed with pencil drawings. There were drawings of animals and apples in bowls, and stones propped against doors. One scene kept recurring – a single tree in a barren wasteland outside a window.

'That was the view from the dormitory at the convent,' Eve said, smiling.

'These are really good, Eve.' I noticed another sketch book inside her bag on the ground beside us. I pulled it out.

'No,' she said, making a grab for the book. 'Not that one.'

I whipped it out of her reach. 'Why?' I said, teasingly. 'What's in it?'

I stood up, holding the book above my head, so she couldn't get at it. She tried to jump up a couple of times, but I could tell she was only half-heartedly trying to stop me.

I grinned and caught her round the waist with my free arm.

'Please may I see?' I said.

She looked up at me. 'OK,' she said. 'But promise you won't laugh.'

I nodded and opened the book.

A picture of a face. A male face.

*Oh my God.*

I stared down at Eve.

# 10

# Personal Jesus

It was my face.

I turned the pages. It was me. Over and over again. Sketched from different angles, and with different expressions. But always, unmistakably, me.

I pored over the drawings. The early ones were a bit rough – I was only just recognisable from the basic shape of the features. But the later ones had more personality, the soft, curving pencil lines making the picture look . . . well, real.

I stopped at one in which I had such a haunted, longing look in my eye you could almost feel it. 'Do I look like that?' I said.

'That was from the last time I saw you. On the beach.' Eve twisted her hair round her finger. 'Or, at least, how I remembered you. Do you . . . ? What do you think?'

'I think they're amazing. I think you're amazing. I had no idea you could draw this well.'

Eve blushed. She gazed far out to sea where the wind had dropped and the water was still. 'There's this one nun at the convent. She really helped with my technique. To be honest, I didn't do much else while I was there.' She paused. 'Of course I couldn't say that these were pictures of you.'

I sat down on the cold grass, still staring at the drawings. The book was full of them. Full of me. It was overwhelming.

'So who did you say I was?' I said.

'I pretended Jesus had come to me in a dream and that's what he looked like.'

I grinned. 'You're kidding.'

Eve smiled back. 'If they knew the truth they'd have stopped me drawing you. It seemed the only option. I told them I'd draw the halo on when I got the face right.'

We both laughed.

'Luke Almighty,' I said. 'That's me. Luke the saviour.'

Eve stopped laughing. 'You did save me,' she said. 'I'd have gone mad if I hadn't known you were out there some-where.'

We stared at each other.

'Still, the convent has done one good thing for me,' Eve said. 'Whatever happens with Mum and Dad, I've decided I'm going to be a graphic designer. I mean I'll still do my own stuff, but I'm also going to art college and train prop-erly so I can get a job.

She looked back at the pictures. 'They're rubbish, really. It was so hard without you being there or without a photograph or anything. Er . . . I was wondering if you'd pose for me actually. So I can draw you from real life.'

'Sure,' I smiled. 'You can do whatever you like with me.' As I leaned across to kiss her, my mobile dug into my hip. Remembering Chloe's call, I removed it from my pocket.

I told Eve what Chloe had said.

Big mistake.

Eve shoved the sketch books back into her bag. I noticed her hands had started trembling again. 'Maybe you should go home, Luke,' she said. 'I feel bad for your mum. And . . .'

'No,' I said. 'Mum's got friends. And Chloe could easily be there if she wanted to be. I'm here with you. For ever.'

I tried to take her hand, but she pulled it away. A tear rolled down her cheek. 'I'm such a mess, Luke,' she said. 'I don't know how I feel about Mum and Dad now – or what I want . . . with . . . when . . .' she tailed off.

'You want *me*, don't you?' I glanced at the sketch book inside her bag. 'Or d'you only want me in two dimensions?'

She shot a look at me. 'I *did* mean what I said,' she

snapped. 'It's just I feel all vulnerable. I don't know if I can.'

I stared at her. *What?* She seemed to have jumped into a whole other conversation.

'If you can what?' I said.

'Do it with you.' Eve said. 'I know I want to. But after last night . . . my dad coming after us . . . everything feels too scary.'

'Oh,' I said, unable to hide the disappointment in my voice. 'Oh.'

'I knew it.' Eve's normally raspy voice rose into a squeak. 'I knew you'd be pissed off.' She stood up and backed away from me, her lips pressed angrily together. 'You're just like all the others.'

'Eve . . .?' I stood up. 'What are you talking about?'

'I might have guessed you'd only come here with me if I promised to . . . to . . . God, I'm so stupid.' Her face twisted with fury. 'I suppose you'll leave now, won't you?'

I stared at her, too shocked for a second to speak. The wind whipped up around us. Just beyond the cliff edge, the waves were ploughing and churning over each other.

And then Eve completely lost it.

'You bastard,' she screamed. 'I bet you've lied about everything. I bet you just told Chloe exactly where I am and—'

'That's so not—'

'So when are you running off home to Mummy?' she yelled, her hands on her hips.

'Stop it,' I shouted. 'I'm not doing any of those things. Why are you—?'

'Right. You're going to phone my dad and tell him where I am, then, aren't you?'

'No.' I stared at her, my breath raging in my throat.

'Yes, you are,' she yelled. 'Because you're scared. You're too frightened to do anything else.'

'Stop it,' I yelled back. How dare she attack me like this when I was here – with her – prepared to do whatever she needed. White-hot anger flooded my head, almost blinding me. I strode across the grass away from her, to the very edge of the cliff. The sea was hurling itself at the jagged grey rocks below. I drew my arm back and flung my mobile as far as I could into the water. There was a tiny splash as it disappeared beneath the waves.

I turned, spreading my arms out wide.

'See?' I yelled. 'I can't call now.' I walked back to her. Our faces were centimetres apart. Her eyes wide and staring. 'I've given up everything,' I said. 'Everything. I don't have anything with me except what I'm wearing. D'you think I'd do that just for a shag?'

I stormed off across the grass, back towards the house.

'Luke.'

Eve ran up beside me, grabbing my arm.

'I'm sorry. I'm sorry.' She pulled at my arm, trying to stop me from walking away. 'Please, I don't know why I said all that. I'm just so scared. I don't know what to do. What's going to happen.' I felt her tugging at my jumper. '*Please*.'

I stopped.

Eve put her arms round me. 'Please. I'm sorry,' she sobbed. 'I didn't mean any of that. I'm just so scared.'

I still felt furious with her. 'You have to trust me,' I spat, my arms at my sides. 'Yes, I want to have sex with you. But I guess I can wait. And yes, I'm scared about what's going to happen to us. But that doesn't mean I'm going to bail on you.'

Eve said nothing, but her whole body was shaking. I could feel her crying into my jumper.

'Listen,' I said more gently, putting my arms around her. 'We'll stay here for a bit. Then we'll find somewhere to work. Somewhere to live. And you can do your training. And . . . and I don't know. We'll just make it work some-how.' I tailed off lamely, but Eve hugged me tighter, still crying.

We stood there for a minute.

I was already regretting having thrown my mobile away.

*Brilliant dramatic gesture, Luke. Next time try throwing something less valuable – like your brain.*

I could feel Eve's tears seeping through my jumper.

'Hey,' I said. 'You're making my chest damp.'

Eve looked up at me, her eyes all red and swollen. She smiled. Then she laughed.

'What?' I said.

'It was funny when you threw your phone in the sea.'

I grinned at her. 'Yeah. Well, at least now your dad won't be able to deploy GPS spy technology to track us down.'

She laughed again.

'Wait here a sec,' she said. She raced across to where she'd been sitting and picked up her bag. Rummaging again, she pulled out an unbranded CD. She walked back towards me in that slightly embarrassed way of hers that I knew so well – her eyes not quite meeting mine, her face just tinged with pink.

'I was wondering if you could input this for me. George's bound to have a computer. Then I could listen to it on your iPod – oh, except . . .' Eve made a face. 'You haven't got your iPod with you, have you? You just said – your phone was the last thing you had.'

The wind whistled around us as I took the CD.

'Actually, I lied,' I grinned. 'My iPod's in my jacket pocket.'

Eve grinned back. 'Just so long as that's all you've lied about.'

Hayley's face flickered across my mind's eye. I blinked her away.

*I didn't lie.*

'How d'you get hold of a CD?' I said.

'One of the girls at the convent has an MP3 player,' Eve said. 'I used to borrow it when I was supposed to be learning Spanish – we used computers for languages. You know, tracks with headphones and stuff. Anyway, there were some songs I really liked. I got her to download them for me onto this.'

'What kind of music is it?' I said.

Eve shrugged. 'Different stuff. Nothing recent. Stuff I like. You'll probably hate it.'

'Why? It's not all slushy love songs, is it?'

'No.'

I grinned as she pretended to hit me.

As we walked back towards the house it struck me that underneath my lust-fuelled love for Eve lay a far simpler feeling.

How much I liked her.

# 11

# Finding music

We went into the kitchen and rooted around for food. Apart from the half-eaten pizza slices and sausage rolls from last night's party, there wasn't much. I found a tin of tuna in one of the cupboards and Eve discovered a half-full jar of mayonnaise and a loaf of slightly stale bread in the fridge.

We made sandwiches and ate them, talking and laughing. Eve seemed much more relaxed since she'd screamed at me outside. I was just about to innocently suggest I showed her our bedroom, when we heard voices in the corridor.

'He threw *what* over the cliff?' This was a girl.

'His phone, Jess,' a male voice replied. 'I saw him from the window. He was yelling and he chucked his mobile into the sea . . .'

I caught Eve's eye. Then the speaker walked into the kitchen. He was about the same age as George, but kind of geeky-looking – curly brown hair and glasses. His mouth fell open when he saw us.

'It's them, Jess!' he turned to the girl coming through the door behind him. She was younger and stockier, with punky hair and enormous black boots.

'Couldn't be bothered to hang on for the upgrade?' she said to me with heavy sarcasm. Then, without waiting for a reply, she stomped over to the kettle and filled it up.

The geeky guy stared at us.

'Hi,' I said. 'I'm Luke. This is Eve.'

I could feel Eve shrinking away again. I reached out and slid my arm round her waist.

The geek was still staring. Then he smiled. 'I'm Cal,' he said.

More voices at the door – and Alejandro and George walked in. Seconds afterwards a bunch of girls appeared, then a few (male) couples whom I avoided looking at. Within minutes the kitchen was full of people. George was clearly in his element. He organised some of the girls to fry bacon and eggs, then pulled a couple of loaves of bread out of the freezer and got one of the guys to make rounds of toast. Soon the kitchen was full of noise and delicious cooking smells.

Cal hovered near us. I could tell he was dying to ask me why I'd thrown my phone into the sea. I eventually suggested to Eve we went up to our room.

Not that I was expecting very much to happen there

now. Surrounded by all those people she had reverted to her earlier state of nervous anxiety and was close to tears again.

Upstairs, we cuddled for a bit, then Eve fell asleep.

Several hours later we came back downstairs to find the house virtually empty. I followed the faint music sounds to the living room. The door to the music room beyond was shut. I glanced sideways at Eve, then opened it.

Rock music blasted out at us. George and Cal were playing guitars and Alejandro was drumming. None of them noticed us come in. Jess, the punky girl from the kitchen was the only other person in the room. She was lying on one of two low sofas in the corner of the room, watching them play. She glanced over at us, unsmiling, then turned back to the music.

We stood for a minute in the doorway. George was bent over his bass, strumming out chords. At last he looked up. He smiled and beckoned us over. I took Eve's hand and dragged her towards the empty sofa. Alejandro grinned at us.

Cal still didn't seem to have noticed we were there.

I sat, transfixed, watching them play. They appeared to be making up what they were doing as they went along – Alejandro just knocking out a steady beat and Cal meandering aimlessly around some tune.

And then something changed. I couldn't tell you what, exactly, but the atmosphere became charged somehow. All three of them started playing with more focus. George frowned with concentration, his fingers changing steadily over and over on the frets of his bass. Alejandro upped the tempo, hitting at the drums more urgently, adding more beats, more rolls. I couldn't separate it out. I couldn't see how they were all playing together without following any music or saying what they were doing.

The music got harder and faster and more insistent. Alejandro was sweating behind his drums, his arms moving so quickly they were almost a blur. George looked over at Cal. Cal nodded. And I realised that somehow they were all communicating with each other.

I sat forwards, completely transfixed by what they were doing – by how it was working. I knew part of it was how hard they were listening to each other but, even so, how did they know what to do next?

Suddenly Cal's guitar broke into an incredible run of chords, his fingers everywhere on the instrument, then slashing down, harder and harder over the strings. The concentration on all their faces increased. Cal was playing like he was about to explode. I could see the others were following him, entirely focused on where he was taking the music.

I could hardly breathe. It was a total adrenalin rush, like my whole body was right there, inside the music, part of it. The sensation wasn't exactly new. Great music was like that, I knew. But this was different because I was so close to it being created. Because I could feel how fragile it was – how easily one wrong note, one wrong beat could bring the whole thing crashing into a tuneless heap. But no one sounded a wrong note or hit an off-beat. At least not as far as I could see.

The music crescendoed furiously. Cal was now clearly oblivious to everything except his guitar. Except I knew he couldn't be. He had to be listening to the others. I wanted to ask him how he got his guitar to make those sounds. How he could play so fast. But I didn't want the music to end.

And then, finally, Cal did look up. Or, it wasn't so much that he looked, as that something shifted in the music and in his body, turning him outwards again. Both George and Alejandro immediately picked up on it – I could hear they were heading to the end.

And then it stopped.

Cal bent over his guitar. George wiped his forehead and grinned at us.

'Fantastic,' he said in his posh voice. ''Cept when Cal went off on that total wank at the end.'

'Piss off,' Cal growled.

'That was good.' Alejandro ran his hand through his hair.

I turned to Eve. But she wasn't there. She must have vanished while I was engrossed in the music. I hadn't even noticed.

'You liked that, Luke?' Alejandro smiled.

I nodded, too overawed to speak.

He came over a few minutes later. 'Is Eva OK?' he said. 'I heard you shouting at each other this morning.'

I blushed.

*Is there anyone here who didn't?*

'I don't know,' I said. 'One minute she's fine, then she gets all upset again.'

Alejandro grimaced. 'I will go and talk with her. Is that all right?'

'Sure.' I smiled at him.

He walked out. A couple of minutes later George left too, muttering something about checking his emails. Jess got up from her sofa and followed him.

Cal was crouching over the guitars laid out by one of the amps. He watched Jess leave, then went back to the instruments.

He'd hardly said a word since they'd stopped playing. I sensed he could have carried on all day. I got up, thinking he didn't look like he wanted any company.

'D'you play?' he said.

I started. 'Er . . . no . . .' I stammered, suddenly nervous. 'I wish I did, though. That was wicked.'

Cal pointed to his guitar. 'Come over here. I'll show you how this thing works.'

I wandered slowly towards him. Why was he showing an interest in me?

He clocked the suspicious look in my eye.

'That blonde your girlfriend?' he said.

I nodded.

Cal's grin deepened. 'Looks like she's worth ditching your mobile for,' he said.

I blushed.

'How d'you pull her, then?'

*Charm. Persistence. A lot of help from Ryan.*

'Luck,' I said.

'Well, it's nice to have someone else straight staying here. I get fed up sometimes with George and his gay army.'

I relaxed a little and reached out for one of the guitars.

'Not that one.' Cal pulled the guitar away. 'That's my Gibson. I had to work for two years to buy it.' He looked round the room, at the guitars spread all over the floor. 'Bloody George has no idea. Gets everything handed to

112

him on a plate. And he'll always get session work no problem, thanks to his dad. Sometimes I hate him.'

He handed me a red guitar from the stack and plugged it in. He showed me how to hold it. 'Now put your fingers here.' He arranged my stiff left-hand fingers across the frets. 'That's E major. Go on. Play.'

I strummed the strings like I'd seen him do. The chord leaped out at me from the amp. I grinned. How cool was that?

'And this is A.' Cal showed me another chord. 'Just keep playing them. One then the other,' Cal said. He tapped his foot slowly on the wooden floor. 'Keep to that rhythm.'

He started playing his Gibson, the music weaving in and out of my single chords. I concentrated as hard as I could. It wasn't easy. Just making my hand strum across the strings evenly was difficult enough, let alone forcing my fingers into the right positions on the frets. After a few minutes, it was easy to lose concentration and let the rhythm slip as well.

Cal stopped after five minutes or so. He smiled at me. 'Not bad,' he said.

I was sure he was just being polite. I knew what I was doing was about the most basic thing in the world, and I was pretty rubbish at even that. But I badly wanted to be better.

'Would you teach me?' I said. 'If you're staying here for a bit and you don't mind.'

Cal nodded. 'Sure. You like it, then – music?'

I thought of Dad and all the records he'd left me when he died – how he'd wanted to show me we were more like each other than I'd realised.

I shrugged. 'Everyone likes music, don't they?'

'Nah. Some people don't. Or they like crap stuff. Or they just pretend to like it. Without really getting it.' He paused. 'They don't know what they're missing. It's better than sex.'

I raised my eyes. 'Maybe you've been screwing the wrong people.'

Cal laughed. 'George would say I've been screwing the wrong sex.' Then his face fell. 'While Jess would point out, very sarcastically, that I haven't been screwing anyone at all.'

He looked so upset for a moment I didn't know what to say. Then he seemed to recover. We talked for a bit longer about the music we liked, then he showed me another couple of chords.

I didn't want to push it, so I left after about half an hour and went off to find Eve.

She seemed more cheerful after her talk with Alejandro. That night, as I fell asleep, I felt as if we'd been staying with George for weeks. Already, the rest of my life – Mum and the baby and Chloe and Ryan, even Jonno – seemed like a dream.

The next few days passed quickly as we settled into the routine of the house. Or, rather, the complete lack of any kind of routine whatsoever. We got up when we felt like it. Ate and drank and slept when we felt like it.

The main shadow over our existence was Jonno. He spent a day calling Alejandro constantly – leaving increasingly irate messages on his voicemail.

Alejandro played me some of them. Jonno sounded insane. Swearing. Threatening us both with everything that occurred to him.

'Sounds like he can't decide whether to torture us before he kills us or just get straight to the decapitation,' I said.

Alejandro sighed. 'Do you think we should play this to Eva?'

'Definitely not,' I said.

Eve was in a terrible state as it was.

She'd wanted to talk to her mum – I think she was hoping to persuade her to stand up to Jonno at last – and had called her from Alejandro's mobile. We were careful not to use a line with a number that could be traced to Cornwall.

She came off the phone in floods of tears. 'Mum was so upset,' she wept in my arms. 'She doesn't understand why I couldn't just stay in Spain for a bit longer. She didn't listen.'

'Don't call her, then,' I said. 'You can email her every now and then to let her know you're OK.'

This was what I'd decided to do with Mum.

The first time I logged on, I found several anxious email messages from her. I think she'd hoped the police would be looking for us and was upset to discover they had better things to do than track down two sixteen-year-olds who were clearly safe and well.

I read all the messages, then sent a short email back:

*Please don't worry. I am fine. We have a place to stay. Just tell Eve's dad you haven't heard from us. I have to help her. Please try and understand.*

Mum then sent me:

*What about school? What about your GCSEs? Come home now.*

To which I replied:

*This is more important.*

This led to a series of far longer emails from Mum detailing why I couldn't – and shouldn't – give up on school before I'd even taken my GCSEs, how there was no way Jonno could take Eve back to Spain if she didn't want to go and that she could go back to her mum's, that we couldn't survive without money, that I mustn't take drugs, that she missed me, that I belonged at home with her and Sam, and – finally – a long, long lecture on not taking risks that could lead to Eve getting pregnant.

Irritated by this last point particularly – for obvious reasons – I shot back:

*Don't you think you're the last person to lecture anyone about unplanned pregnancies?*

Which did not go down well.

After that I only contacted her every few days to let her know I was still alive and OK. I didn't open any more of her emails and after a week or so she stopped sending them.

It was a weird existence. We never left the house. Cal and Jess were there most of the time and there was a steady stream of other people who dropped in and out. George went out occasionally, coming back very late at night and crashing around the house, waking everyone up.

He was unbelievably generous to us. He ordered on-line food deliveries every few days so there was always masses to eat and he even lent me some of his old clothes. In fact, Eve and I didn't have to worry about anything. Looking back, I don't think it occurred to me just how hard it would have been if he hadn't taken us in like he did. We tried to do things back for him. Eve cooked most evenings, usually with Jess glowering at her from across the kitchen. She and I painted a couple of bedrooms – jobs that were on the long 'to do' list George's parents had left him. And I did some other work round the house too – stuff Dad had shown me how to do a few years ago.

I thought about him a lot . . . my dad, I mean. Part of me felt angry with him for not being around – I think that was because I felt guilty about leaving Mum on her own. Part of me just wished I could show him all the practical stuff I was doing.

I could remember so clearly being irritated when I was younger and he'd insist on teaching me how to replace a fuse and saw a plank of wood and use a rawlplug to fix a shelf bracket. It was hard, now, to do those same things and not be able to show him that I had been listening after all.

George was particularly impressed when I put up some shelves in the garage.

'You're amazing, Luke,' he said. 'So many hidden talents.'

I always had the impression that he was flirting with me – which made me feel very uncomfortable.

'But he's like that with everyone,' Eve pointed out.

It was true. George was a total party animal – at the centre of everything that happened in the house, with apparently limitless supplies of money and good humour. I often caught him staring at Eve with a puzzled expression on his face, but he never pushed us about our situation or implied there was a limit to the length of time we could stay with him.

Eve seemed to get stronger as the days passed. She spent most of her time sketching and flatly refused Alejandro's suggestion she try singing with him and the others. Her dad had made her sing with the nightclub band at his hotel in the summer and Eve had hated it. She loved me playing the guitar, though – said it really suited me – and listened to me every day while I practised.

The only person who was at all difficult about us being in the house was Jess. Ugly, unsmiling and rude – I disliked her intensely and I knew Eve did too. She hardly said a word to us. But then she didn't speak to anyone really, except for George, whom she followed round like a shadow.

I didn't understand their relationship. Well. They didn't have one. That is, Jess was clearly crazy about George. But he didn't seem to notice.

'Oh, he knows,' Alejandro had said, when Eve asked him about it. 'He is just not interested.'

'Course not,' I said when Eve told me. 'He's gay and she's horrible.'

Eve shrugged, then explained to me that Alejandro had also told her Cal was in love with Jess.

'What?' I said. 'Why?'

Neither of us could understand it.

Cal seemed as unable to leave Jess as Jess did George. I had no idea what either of their home situations was, and neither of them ever said.

So, with Eve drawing and me learning to play the guitar, we stayed at the house in Cornwall for another two weeks.

And, no, we still hadn't had sex.

# 12

# More than music

Alejandro had been back in Spain for several days when he
called to tell us he'd seen Jonno.

'He arrived at my gig in Madrid,' he explained. '*Mierda*.
At first I thought he was going to kill me, but the whole
band were there so he just shouted. He was so cross about
Eva and what you did to his car. I told him that I gave Eva
money and left you both at a train station in Somerset. I
said I had no idea where you are now. I think he believed
me.'

I reported this conversation to Eve.

'D'you think that means Dad's given up looking for us?'

'For now, maybe,' I said.

But I couldn't imagine Jonno ever really giving up. The
murderous way he'd looked at me when he'd seen me in
that hotel car park went too deep for that. I knew that I was
different from Alejandro in his eyes. As far as Jonno was
concerned I'd done something worse than help Eve run

away from him – I'd stopped her being his little girl. I didn't think he'd ever let that go.

It was ironic, I thought, that Jonno was probably imagining me seducing Eve on a daily basis when, in fact, although we slept in the same bed, Eve was careful never to let things go too far.

She talked about it a lot, reassuring me how much she wanted me, saying over and over how she just needed a little more time – how the fact that we were actually doing less than we had been in the summer was because she knew how easy it would be for her to get carried away.

None of this made any sense to me. She said she wanted me more than she ever had. And I knew she wasn't lying. Every little thing I did turned her on more – far more – than it used to. So why was she holding back?

'It's only until I feel safe,' she'd say. 'Not so up and down all the time.'


When I wasn't with Eve, I spent most of my time with Cal. He gave me daily guitar lessons and got me totally caught up in his music. I loved listening to him – the more I learned about playing the guitar, the more I admired his skill and the way he made what he did look so effortless. Sometimes he even let me play with him and George – though I noticed he always turned my amp right down.

I practised until my fingers bled.

Eve sat outside every morning, sketching and listening to me playing, or to the music from her CD that I'd imported onto my iPod. She stayed in the cold for hours, drawing the cliffs and the sea and the trees. Inside, she just drew me. The others teased her about that, saying she should try sketching them too, but Eve always shook her head. 'Not until I get this right,' she'd say. 'I don't know what I'm doing wrong, but it's not really Luke.'

'Yeah, you've made him way too fit,' George would say, winking at me.

Sometimes I thought about Mum, or school. But not often. It was too easy here just to drift from one day to the next. Eating when I got hungry, playing the guitar and being with Eve.

Alejandro came back from Spain just before the end of January. His tour was finished and he had a week before he went home to do some work for his dad.

Late one morning, towards the end of that week, Alejandro, Eve and I were in the kitchen making toast when George and Cal strolled in.

'Guess what?' George grinned. 'Cal and I have got a gig. This friend of my dad just called – been let down last minute. We have to be in London for tomorrow evening.'

They started talking about the detail of the job. It was going to last a week.

Eve put down her spoon and looked at me.

'Er . . . George,' I said. 'What about us?'

His green eyes sparkled as he took in our anxious faces. 'Well . . .' he said slowly.

'George, behave.' Alejandro smiled.

'Yes, George, stop winding them up,' Cal said irritably.

George chuckled. 'My parents have this place in the West End,' he said. 'I think I told you about it. It's not big and there's no soundproofing which is why I don't use it more, but there's room for you two to stay there with us if you want.'

*Yes.* However much I liked being here with Eve and playing the guitar, going back to London meant a chance to see Mum and our friends and maybe even a chance to work out what Eve and I were going to do next.

'What about Jess?' Cal said in an ultra-casual voice that fooled no one.

George groaned. 'No, she can't come too. There's not enough room. C'mon, Cal, surely you can tear yourself away for a few days? It's not as if anything's going to happen.'

Cal stood up and walked off. Alejandro followed him.

'Bloody hell.' George wrinkled his nose. 'Was it something I said?'

Eve smiled at him.

'You'd think the way he plays he could get anyone into bed,' George sighed. 'Still, I guess it takes more than music.'

Alejandro reappeared at the door. 'What takes more than music?' he said.

'Shagging, baby,' George said. He sat up. 'Hey! Party. Tonight.'

He swept out.

Eve and I exchanged glances. This wasn't the first time we'd seen George get all excited about having a party in the morning, only to see the whole thing fizzle out into a few of his mates coming round for pizza and beer.

But today turned out to be different. George texted some friends, who called other friends. By 10.30 pm, a steady stream of people had started trickling into the house.

Eve took a long time getting ready. When she emerged from the bathroom along our corridor my mouth fell open, she looked so amazing. Normally she just wore jeans – she'd only brought a few clothes with her – but tonight she had on this little skirt I hadn't seen before.

'George gave it to me,' she said. 'He said it was his sister's from before she left home.'

I snorted. 'From before she went to secondary school, you mean.'

The skirt was tiny.

'Don't you like it?' Eve's face fell.

By the time I'd told her exactly how much I liked it the party was in full swing.

Alejandro, George and Cal played with a girl singer who wore low-cut jeans with a snake tattoo creeping out of them up her back and round to her stomach. I thought it was kind of sexy. Eve wrinkled up her nose.

'But think how that snake head'll look if she gets fat,' she said.

I grinned and pulled her up off the sofa to dance.

More people arrived at midnight, including one of George's DJ friends, who set himself up in the music room with his massive decks and four huge boxes of vinyls.

Cal looked deeply uncomfortable as soon as he stopped playing his Gibson. He sat slumped on one of the sofas, staring at Jess dancing with some of George's friends. George, of course, threw himself totally into the party – providing more and more drink and dancing more and more outrageously.

I was chatting with Alejandro about some music we were both into, when a dance track came on I recognised from Eve's CD.

Eve appeared from nowhere. She grabbed my hand and dragged me off to dance. The music pounded in our ears, a fast, pulsing beat above a low, growling bass. It was one of my favourite tracks off Eve's selection and it sounded fantastic played so loud, filling the entire room. We danced like we were on fire, our arms twisting round each other, our bodies moving perfectly together.

The music was outside and inside me at the same time. My whole body filled with happiness – I closed my eyes, totally caught up in the mood of the music, completely blissed-out at being here with Eve.

I felt her moving closer, her body rolling against mine. I opened my eyes.

*I want you.*

We stared at each other – still somehow moving in this perfect rhythm.

And then she nodded.

And I knew that she meant she was ready. Now. It was time.

My throat tightened. After nearly four weeks of her being so uncertain, I was scared that as soon as we were away from the charged party atmosphere, she would change her mind again.

George's words from this morning went through my head. *'It takes more than music.'*

Or maybe music was exactly what it took. The dance track thudded in my ears. Maybe if I could keep it alive in her head, I could keep her wanting me. Wanting *it*. I leaned over her shoulder and drew my iPod out of my pocket. Still dancing, I switched on the backlight.

Where the hell was the track we were listening to? I found *Eve's playlist*. There. Now what followed it? It had to be right. *Yes.* Perfect. The next song was a total make-out track if ever I'd heard one – and then two really sexy ballads. Ones I knew Eve loved.

As soon as the music in the room ended, I held up the iPod, the headset in my hands. Eve stared at me as I fitted the earphones into her ears, then smiled as she realised the same track was now playing through the MP3 player.

I took her hand and guided her across the heaving dance floor. I had the iPod in my hand, careful not to move too suddenly and jerk the ear phones out of Eve's ears. Somehow knowing we were connected like that added to how horny the whole thing was.

Through the music room, the living room, the corridor. It felt completely different out here – the music from the deck now only a background sound. People were scattered about on the stairs – talking, kissing. *Oh God.* There were boys snogging each other. Tongues and everything. I shuddered and glanced quickly at Eve. She didn't seem to have noticed. The track we'd been dancing to was still playing in her ears.

She nodded again.

I put my arm round her and we climbed the stairs. Two minutes later we were back in our room. As soon as I'd shut the door Eve started kissing me. *Mmmn.* She was moving in time with the music in her head, really into what we were doing. Which was great. Except I had the iPod in my hand and she was pulling me towards the bed and I had to keep checking I wasn't jerking the earphones out.

I lay down carefully beside her. More kissing. *Yes.* It was working. The whole music thing was definitely working. Although.

*Damn.*

There was no way I was going to be able to get her top over her head without dislodging the earphones. Sighing, I rolled it up as far as I could – which wasn't very far – then I kissed her stomach, trying to be as careful as possible not to knock the iPod wire with my elbow.

This wasn't exactly the abandoned sexual experience I'd been looking forward to. More than half my mind was still on the stupid machine lying beside me. Why hadn't I thought to bring a CD player up here? Or proper stay-on headphones?

I heard the dance track finish and prayed that the segue to the love song wouldn't make her want to stop.

It didn't. In fact it turned her on more. Her breath quickened into gasps and she pulled me higher and closer. I felt her fingernails scraping against my chest as she unbuttoned my shirt.

Suddenly worrying about the iPod earphones falling out of her ears faded to the back of my mind.

*I want this.*

I kept my eyes fixed on hers while my hands moved down, willing her not to lose faith in me.

I was so close to her now I could hear the whole song in her ears. She was so beautiful, gazing up at me all trusting and loving and right.

I reached under the mattress for where I'd stashed the condoms I'd nicked weeks ago out of George's bathroom.

'I love you,' I mouthed.

Eve smiled back and I felt her hands tugging at my jeans. And my heart started pounding and she was only centimetres away and the look in her eyes said it was OK and suddenly I knew I couldn't wait much longer.

And then she stopped and took the earphones out.

'It's so special that it's us . . . that we're together doing this.' She looked right into my eyes. 'For our first time.'

For a fraction of a second I remembered Hayley.

I looked away. *No.*

*Shit.*

Eve had seen.

I knew she'd seen.

Her hands were on my face, pushing it round, forcing me to look at her again. Her mouth was open, her eyes wide, uncomprehending.

I could feel my cheeks burning.

The music was hissing away through the earphones on the bed beside us. The faint thump of the latest dance track playing downstairs the only other sound.

*It was nothing. It was nothing. It was nothing.*

Eve backed away from me, pulling the covers over her.

'Who was she?' she whispered.

'No one. Nothing. What d'you mean?' I said.

I could hear how pathetic I sounded.

'I saw in your eyes.' Eve's lips trembled. 'You promised me you hadn't . . . you said you didn't go out with anyone while . . . when I wasn't here.'

I stared at her.

*No. Not this. Not now. Not* now.

'Luke.' She swore. 'Tell me what happened.'

So I told her. In about three sentences. An edited version, obviously, emphasising how Ryan had totally set me up and how Hayley had virtually forced herself on me when it was the last thing I expected.

'I thought she just wanted me to walk with her because . . . because it was late.'

'You went with her to an empty apartment in the middle

of the night?' Eve stared at me incredulously. 'What did you *think* was going to happen?'

I couldn't bring myself to explain about the fish-checking scenario I had totally bought into at the time. 'It wasn't planned,' I stammered. 'I didn't even like her much.'

Eve's whole face screwed up in puzzlement. 'You slept with her and you didn't like her? How is that possible?'

I had no idea what to say. 'I don't know.'

Tears welled in Eve's eyes. 'I can't believe you lied to me. I specifically asked you when I saw you that first night. You—'

'I didn't lie to you,' I said desperately. 'The whole time you were gone I thought about you all the time. I didn't see anyone I wanted to talk to. Or anyone I wanted at all.'

'Except her.' Eve's lips set together in a thin line. Her breath sounded fast and harsh. 'She must have been special.'

'No, she wasn't. God, Eve, we didn't go out with each other. It was just that one time. It didn't mean anything.'

I reached out for her hand but she sat up in the bed, pulling the covers tightly around her. My iPod slid further away from us, down the bed.

'That's what you said about Catalina,' she said. 'Did you like this *other* girl as much as that?'

*Shit.* Catalina was this incredibly fit Spanish girl I'd got

132

off with in the summer when Eve had temporarily dumped me.

'No. Yes. I don't know. It wasn't important. *She* wasn't important. You're the one and only—'

'How could it not be important?' Eve frowned, her voice cracking. 'Didn't you want it to be important? Didn't you want it to be special?'

I reached out again, now trying to touch her face.

'It would be special with you,' I said helplessly.

'Get off me,' Eve snarled.

'Please, Eve,' I said. 'I didn't know if you were coming back. Remember – you said you'd understand.'

'Get out.' Eve kicked at me under the bed covers. 'GET OUT,' she shouted.

'But—'

'ARE YOU DEAF? GET OUT!' she yelled.

Grabbing my shirt off the bed, I stumbled to the door. As I walked out into the corridor landing, I could hear Eve slam it shut behind me.

I sank down onto the floor, totally numb.

Inside the room, I could hear Eve starting to cry.

# 13

# After the party

I was still sitting in the corridor half an hour later. The party was going strong – the music thumping up through the floorboards.

Alejandro appeared, heading towards his own room opposite. His eyes widened when he saw me. 'Luke?' he said. 'What's happened?'

'Nothing.' I tried to smile at him. 'I'm fine.'

Alejandro stared at me. 'If so fine, why are you in the corridor?'

I shrugged and leaned back against the wall.

'Is it Eva?' Alejandro rolled his eyes. '*Mierda*. Let me talk to her.'

He knocked softly on our door. 'Eva?'

She let him in. I could hear them talking in low voices.

I sat hunched over, wondering what he was saying.

Wondering how on earth how I was going to get Eve to understand that what I'd done with Hayley meant nothing.

Alejandro's voice got louder. '*Hijo de* . . . Eva. What did you *expect* him to do? He did not know when he would see you again.'

Eve said something I couldn't hear.

'Of course it doesn't,' Alejandro said. 'He is sixteen. You expect him to act like he is married to you.'

I didn't hear any more. A couple of minutes later Alejandro re-emerged.

I looked up at him. He shook his head. 'Now she hates me too,' he said. 'I think it is better to wait. Talk in the morning.'

He went back downstairs.

In spite of what Alejandro had said, I waited outside the room, hoping Eve would open the door. As the night went on, more people wandered up the stairs. Most of them were vaguely recognisable to me as members of what Cal had referred to as George's 'gay army'. Several were in pairs, clearly looking for a bit more privacy than they were getting on the stairs or in the kitchen. Others were yawning and alone, just trying to find somewhere to crash.

They all stared at me.

Some of them hopefully.

I got up and found another room to sleep in.

The house was a total mess in the morning – far worse than on the day we'd arrived, after the New Year party. Cal woke a grumbling George at eleven, pointing out we needed to set off for London in an hour. He forced George to chivy all the overnight guests out of the house. He even made him leave twice the normal fee for the cleaner who came every week.

Eve refused to talk to me, or even look at me.

She emerged from our room, pale and red-eyed and went straight up to George to ask him if she could ride in his car to London. We had planned to drive up together with Alejandro.

'Luke's not coming with us to the flat any more,' she announced loudly. 'He's going home.'

I saw Cal and George exchange meaningful looks. My stomach twisted into a knot. This was it – she was dumping me.

I couldn't bear it.

Eve made up with Alejandro, thanking him effusively for all the help he'd given her and promising to pay him back for everything he'd done. But she still refused to listen to anything he said about me.

'She says it is no so much you sleeping with this girl,' Alejandro explained as we drove up the motorway in his car. 'More that you lied about it. She says she cannot trust you any more.'

I looked out of the window. 'Why won't she let me speak to her?'

Alejandro glanced sideways at me. 'She says she is scared of being weak. She says she loves you too much. Wants you too much. She is worried she will go back to you, if she lets you ask her.'

I groaned. But this did give me some hope – until I started stressing about whether Cal would try to take advantage of Eve being miserable by hitting on her.

'I doubt it.' Alejandro shook his head. 'Cal loves his guitar more than a girl. And his head is full of Jess anyway. George though . . . this is the perfect situation for him.'

I frowned. 'I thought George was gay?'

Alejandro laughed. 'George is whatever will get him to the sex fastest. There is a good word in English for him. Hedonist.'

I stared at him blankly.

'Enjoys everything. That is George.' Alejandro tapped lightly on the steering wheel. Then he grinned at me. 'You should go back to school, Luke. Learn more words.'

By the time we reached London I'd decided – on Alejandro's advice – to let Eve alone for a couple of days, then go round and try talking to her again. Alejandro gave me the address of George's flat, then dropped me in Central London.

Unhappy and anxious, I took the tube home, arriving

back as I'd left – only without my phone or my iPod, which I had left in our room and which Eve hadn't returned to me that morning.

I'd lost my key somewhere in Cornwall so I had to ring the doorbell. It was about six pm and raining. Despite dreading the fury I was sure Mum was about to unleash on me, I hoped she was in.

I was cold and hungry.

But Mum didn't open the door. Trisha did, baby Sam in her arms.

She did a double-take when she saw me. 'Luke?'

'Hi.' I smiled. 'Is Mum here?'

Trisha frowned at me. 'Of course. God, Luke, where've you been?'

I walked past her, ignoring the question. I looked round. It felt weird being home. After a month away everything looked familiar and yet somehow really strange as well.

'Luke.' Trisha sounded cross.

I spun round. Little Alice was running across the hall towards me. She hugged my leg. I bent down and picked her up. 'Hey, Alice.'

She grinned.

'Luke.' Trisha was staring at me, this hard look in her eyes. 'I need to talk to you before you see your mum.'

I shrugged and followed her into the living room. I sat in Dad's old armchair, Alice on my lap. Trisha perched on the sofa opposite, jiggling Sam over her shoulder, her face all serious.

'I can't believe you strolling in here like nothing's happened,' she said. 'I thought you were more . . . more grown up than that.'

A knot of anger tightened in my chest. I set Alice down on the floor, then pushed myself up off the chair.

I was going to get enough of a bollocking from Mum. I didn't need this.

'Listen to me,' Trisha said, furiously. 'Your mother's in a terrible state. Today's not a bad day – at least she got dressed. But she's still upstairs right now, in her room.'

'What?' I sat back down in the chair, a flicker of worry filtering through my anger. 'What's the matter with her?'

Trisha rolled her eyes. 'She's depressed, Luke. Real, serious depression. She wasn't good anyway, before you went. But now . . .'

'Because I went away?' I frowned. 'But I sent emails. I made sure she knew I was OK.'

'For goodness sake,' Trisha snapped. 'She didn't know where you were. You're sixteen. Still at school. Or supposed to be. Anything could have been happening to you. And I heard your girlfriend's father on the phone. He was

terrifying. *And* the school called *and* social services . . .
Chloe'd only just moved out too, remember.'

I stared at her.

'And then, as if all that wasn't enough, Matt left her. Just
walked out one evening saying it was over.'

'*What?*'

'Yeah. I came round about a week after you'd gone,
to see how she was. I was worried because she hadn't
answered my calls. He'd left her the day before. Almost
exactly one year to the day since your dad died.'

*Oh God.* I hadn't even thought about the date Dad died.
I put my head in my hands. I knew how much that would
have upset Mum. And I hadn't been here. I hadn't even
called.

Trisha appeared to be reading my mind.

'That's right, Luke,' she said. 'Your mum was all alone.
When I came round she was like this half-dead person. She
hadn't eaten, hadn't got up, hadn't washed. She'd dragged
herself out of bed to feed the baby. But . . .' Trisha's face
crumpled. 'I didn't know what to do. I called out the doctor
and he gave her some pills and they're supposed to start
working soon. I wanted her to come to mine but she
wouldn't. So I've been living here since.' Her voice rose to
a shout. 'And it's not fair. I'm a single mum and I'm eight-
and-a-half months sodding pregnant!'

'What about Chloe?' I stammered.

Trisha sighed as if she was too exhausted to keep on being angry. 'She's come round a few times, but to be honest I don't think she helps. It's not as if they even get on that well.' She looked up at me. 'It's you she wants to see. You she's been worried about.'

I sat back in the armchair, guilt flooding through my veins like ice water.

# 14

# Out of reach

Trisha went up first to say I was back.

I heard Mum call out my name and I ran up the stairs three at a time. She was sitting on her bed, her face haggard, her hair all lank and straggly, her clothes creased and crumpled.

Tears leaked out of her eyes when she saw me. I hugged her, my insides turning over and over. I'd never seen her look like this.

She stroked my hair, whispering my name.

'I'm sorry, Mum.' I was seriously close to crying as she buried her face in my shoulder. 'I'm sorry.'

She felt so fragile. So broken.

I wanted her to forgive me. To say that everything was all OK now. To say that she was fine, now that I was back. But when she looked up at me, her eyes were dull . . . empty.

'Mum?'

She was looking at me, but it was like she wasn't really seeing me. Like there was this barrier between us.

I held her, reassuring her I was fine. I had expected her to be angry or, at least, to demand a hundred explanations from me about what I'd been doing.

But she didn't shout or ask me any questions. Not even about Eve.

It was like she was Mum and yet not Mum, at the same time. It was creepy and sad and really, really scary.

Trisha tried to explain it to me later. 'It's like she's in this black box, and she can't get out of it back into her life. The anti-depressants will help soon, though, I hope. And you being back is the most important thing, Luke. She doesn't have anyone else.'

My heart slid into my gut. I didn't want this. My whole plan coming home had been to give Eve a few days, then get her to take me back. Back to Cornwall. Back to the guitar. Back to our life. Yes, and back to the sex I still hadn't had.

But how could I go back now?

Dads. It all came down to them. If mine hadn't died then Mum wouldn't be in this state. And if Eve's wasn't a total whack job, she and I would have been together all autumn and Hayley could never have happened.

*

Ryan came round on Sunday afternoon. We'd texted each other a few times when Eve and I were in Cornwall – I'd borrowed George's phone – but it was kind of weird seeing him again

He asked for a beer as soon as he arrived. I found a stash in one of the kitchen cupboards and took it out to the garden. We were sitting outside to get away from Sam's crying – which had graduated from the old mewing squeal to a piercing scream.

Ryan drank the beer quickly while I told him about Eve.

'Why didn't you just lie about Hayley?' he asked, looking staggered by my stupidity.

I shrugged. 'Dunno. Eve just knew. Without me saying anything.'

Ryan set down his empty bottle on the grass and laughed. 'So correct me if I'm wrong, but that means that you managed to get Hayley into bed in about five seconds flat, whereas you've been living with Eve – your mind-reading girlfriend – for a month and it still hasn't happened?'

*Piss off, Ryan.*

'What about you?' I said, pointedly changing the subject.

'This and that,' he said, smugly. He raised his eyebrows, obviously hoping I'd ask more questions so he could boast

144

about however many girls it was he'd shagged since I last saw him.

I suddenly didn't want to hear it.

'Chloe's coming over later,' I said. 'D'you want to stay?'

A weird expression crossed Ryan's face. Sort of scared and hurt and worried all at once. He stood up. 'No. Er . . . I need to get going anyway. I'm meeting someone.'

'What's going on with you two?' I said. 'When did you actually last see each other?'

'Mmmn.' Ryan wouldn't meet my eyes. 'Well, I may have failed to fill you in on all the details when we . . . er . . . last time we spoke . . .'

'What d'you mean?'

Ryan grinned. But the smile looked forced. 'We broke up. Actually, she dumped me that night your mum had the baby.'

'What? Why didn't you say anything?' I could feel my mouth hanging open and made no attempt to close it.

'Didn't want everyone making a big deal about it.' Ryan shrugged. 'Like you are now. Look, it's fine. I'm fine about it.'

'But . . . but . . .' I stared at him. He did sound totally unbothered, as if he was chatting about a couple of football teams he was vaguely interested in. And yet, why wasn't he looking properly at me?

'Aren't you upset?' I said. *Being without Eve is killing me.*

'No way.' Ryan stared at the grass. 'It's given me a chance to see all sorts of girls. You know how I once had a thing with Kelly Simmonds? Well, she's got a friend who—'

'Hold on, Ry. Stop.' I frowned, still failing to get my head around Ryan's cheerful tone. 'So you're *pleased* about being dumped, then?'

'It's not a big deal,' he said, his voice still all casual. Then he met my eyes at last. Just for a couple of seconds. But it was enough.

He walked off. I stared after him, shocked.

Not by what he'd said. But by the amount of hurt in his eyes. Hurt that he hadn't been able to hide.


Half an hour later, the phone rang.

Trisha was out with Alice doing some food shopping and I knew from the last twenty-four hours that Mum hardly ever answered the phone any more.

I picked up the receiver. 'Hi.'

There was a fierce intake of breath and then an explosion.

'You sodding little shit. I'm going to kill you when I get my hands on you. Where is she? Is she with you now?'

146

Jonno.

I was so shocked that I slammed the phone down.

It rang again immediately. I let it ring a few times, then realised if I didn't answer it Mum might – and I didn't want Jonno shouting at her. I picked the phone up.

'Don't you dare hang up on me again,' Jonno roared. 'Where's Eve?'

I gulped. 'I don't know,' I said. This was technically true. The piece of paper on which Alejandro had written her address was screwed up in my jeans pocket. I had no idea what it said.

'Don't lie to me, you evil piece of—'

'I really don't know,' I said, loudly. 'She dumped me. That's why I'm here. At home.'

Silence. I waited while the non-psychotic part of Jonno's brain processed this information. The last thing I wanted was to give him the satisfaction of thinking Eve no longer wanted me. But this was the only way I could think of getting him off my back. Off Mum's back.

'Hah.' Jonno sucked in his breath again. 'Came to her senses then, did she? Realised she can do better?'

'I suppose so.' I made rude signs with my fingers at the phone.

*Actually she's now shacked up with a bisexual bass player and an obsessive rock guitarist.*

147

'But I don't think she wants to go back to that prison you kept her in in Spain,' I added.

'No.' Jonno's voice suddenly sounded unbearably heavy and sad. 'Well, just so long as she's not with you,' he growled.

There was a long pause.

'Right,' I said.

'Listen.' Jonno was making chewing noises. I guessed he had a cigar in his mouth. I could just picture him – slicked-back hair, gold jewellery and that handsome, wasted face. 'D'you know if she's OK? I mean for money? It's just I was worried that she might not have enough. I know Alejandro's helping her. To be honest that's the only reason why I didn't beat him to a pulp in Madrid – but he won't . . . he can't do it for ever. And I know how easy it is to get into trouble when you're broke.' He stopped.

This uneasy feeling twisted into my stomach.

He cared about her. Yeah, he hated me and he didn't want to let Eve live her own life and all that, but deep down he cared.

'Luke?'

'Yeah. Er . . . I think she's fine. For money, I mean.'

'Good.'

Another long pause.

'And if you do see her, tell her I'm here. If she wants to call.'

The line went dead.

I put the receiver down slowly.

# 15

# Not talking

'It's a trick,' Chloe said, several hours later. 'He wants you to make Eve think he's changed so he can kidnap her again and send her back to that hellhole in Spain.'

We were discussing Jonno's call with Trisha while Alice ate fishfingers at the kitchen table. Sam was grizzling in Chloe's arms. Trisha was standing at the counter, heating up a bottle of milk for him.

I shook my head. 'Maybe he realises now he went too far.'

Chloe snorted and pinched one of Alice's fishfingers.

'Hey, they're mine,' Alice said.

'You have to learn to share.' Chloe licked her fingers.

'I expect it's a mix of things,' Trisha said, looking irritatedly at Chloe. 'I mean he's bound to be worried. He's her dad.' She handed Chloe the warmed-up milk.

Chloe waved the bottle in the air. 'Like Matt's worried about Sam?' she said.

We all stared at the baby. He had changed a lot since I'd left at Christmas. His face was rounder and fuller – more like a proper baby's face. He was still scarily small, but he did look a lot cuter than he had five weeks ago.

'How could anyone leave him?' Trisha murmured.

When Alice finished her tea, Trisha took her upstairs for a bath. Mum appeared and sat with us for a while. Then she went up to change Sam's nappy.

'Mum seems a lot better,' Chloe said.

I stared at her. 'You're kidding.'

Chloe rolled her eyes. 'You have no idea, Luke. It was hell here.'

'Hell for Trisha, maybe,' I said. 'You weren't here.'

'Neither were you,' she snapped. She stood up. 'I'm going now. Gotta get back to the house.'

I stared at her. 'So how is it? You know, work and your flat-share.'

Chloe looked at me suspiciously. 'There's no spare room,' she said.

'Jesus Christ, Chlo. I'm not trying to muscle in on your fabulous new life,' I said. 'It's just I saw Ry earlier. He . . .'

I stopped. Chloe's expression had changed. The hard, ironic glare in her eye that was there almost all the time, had gone. She looked suddenly vulnerable. Like she wasn't much older than Alice.

'Ry was here?' she said, in a tiny voice.

'Yeah. He . . . look, Chlo, I know it's none of my business, but what *happened*?'

I half expected Chloe to flounce indignantly out of the room. But instead she sank back into the kitchen chair and sighed.

'I thought I wanted all this other stuff. Like work,' she said. 'I mean, I hated school. But to be honest that stupid shop isn't any better. In fact it's worse. Well, worse than English anyway. You can't turn up late and there are all these fascists there telling you what to do and it's so boring. I mean it's great having the money and the flat, but otherwise . . . ?'

'But what about Ryan?' I said.

Above our heads I could hear Alice squealing as Trisha ordered her out of the bath.

Chloe sighed again. 'I thought I wanted to be on my own.' She paused. 'Well. Really I thought I wanted the chance to go out with other guys. But . . .' she looked down at the floor.

'But they didn't ask you out?' I grinned.

She narrowed her eyes at me. 'You are such a bin-licker. No. They're just not him, that's all.' And she got up and stomped out of the kitchen.

\*

The next day was Monday. I went back to school. It was weird being there after so many weeks away. I was hauled into the head's office first thing and given an hour-long bollocking for running away and truanting and being immature and generally excessively stupid. 'And in your GCSE year as well, Luke,' she said.

As if doing it at some other time would have been fine.

I was told I would have to do loads of extra work to catch up. And that it was only my home circumstances – dead dad, mad mum, though that's not how they put it – that had persuaded them against permanently excluding me.

I sat there, taking it, feeling resentful and sulky. Three days ago I'd been living in a great house, learning to play the guitar from a genius guitar player. And Eve had loved me.

*Eve.*

Whenever I thought about her it hurt in the pit of my stomach. I had her address. I could go round. I should, maybe, to tell her about Jonno's phone call. I knew Cal and George weren't going to be here very long. In a week's time she'd probably be back in Cornwall, hundreds of miles away.

But I was scared to see her. Not just because she might not take me back. But in case she did. And then I would face a choice I didn't want to make.

Eve or Mum.

On Wednesday, Trisha told me that she was going to move back home at the weekend. 'I can't stay here any longer, Luke,' she said. 'I need to get the place ready for the new baby. And it's starting to affect Alice being here all the time. And your Mum's getting better now.'

It was true. Mum did seem a bit better. The dead look in her eye had lifted a little and she got up more and came downstairs. She'd even asked me about Eve and where we'd stayed. I knew she wanted to ask me about how far we'd gone together – and other stuff too, about drugs and money. I gave her a few, broad reassurances: I'm not a junkie; I'm not a thief. Then made it clear I didn't want to talk. She didn't push it.

I started fantasising about getting Eve back and going down to Cornwall again. 'Maybe Mum'll be OK on her own?' I said.

Trisha shook her head. 'I know it's not fair, Luke. It should be Matt here dealing with all this. But he isn't. And it's not as if there's really somewhere else you should be. You're still at school. This is where you belong.'

And so the week slid away.

Cal called me on Thursday and told me to come over to George's flat that evening for a guitar session. 'You gotta practise every day,' he said. 'Or you'll slip back.'

'Will Eve be there?' I didn't know whether I wanted him to say yes or no.

'Nah.' I could hear Cal plucking at his Gibson, his mind only half on our conversation. 'She's going out. With George.'

I wanted to ask him what he meant. Going out how? Out buying food? Out on a date? Out shagging each other senseless on a park bench somewhere?

But Cal just hung up, with a final reminder to come round at seven.

Anyway, as I put down the phone I reflected that George didn't need to take Eve outside to have sex with her. She was living in his freaking flat. In fact, when I thought about it, she was completely dependent on him. He could force her to do what he liked, couldn't he? *Sleep with me, Eve, or you're out on the street.*

My head pulsed with rage for a few minutes, until it occurred to me that if George had wanted to blackmail either of us like that he would have done it a month ago. No. He was basically a nice bloke. Spoilt rotten of course, with all that money and his big home. And a bit weird, maybe. Certainly far too touchy-feely with guys for my liking. But he was fun and generous and . . . *God* . . . Eve wouldn't go for him, would she?

I was there, knocking on the door, at five to seven.

\*

George's flat was in Kensington – a plush apartment full of expensive-looking furniture and crowded with ornaments, just like the house in Cornwall.

Cal had set the amps up in the living room. He let me borrow his old guitar – a third-hand Flying V. I was dying to ask him about George and Eve, but it wasn't easy. Cal basically had three topics of conversation. Rock music. His Les Paul Gibson guitar. And how poor he was. He did, apparently, sometimes talk about Jess and his undying love for her – but he'd never done that with me and he didn't start that night.

Instead I had to endure two hours of exactly why his Les Paul was the best in the world. I'd heard it all before. Many times. I tried to focus on the music and the Flying V in my hands.

Playing again was fantastic. My fingers slid over the frets easily now. It was almost impossible to remember how stiff and awkward they'd felt at first. We worked on some of our favourite stuff, then tried out a couple of new tracks Cal had written.

I got totally lost in the music, not thinking about what I had to do next, just going with it, letting it flow, listening to how Cal was improvising around me.

We stopped for a beer. I caught Cal looking at me with an expression that might almost have been pride. 'You're not bad, now, you know,' he said gruffly. 'Might even let you try out my Gibson someday soon.'

This was about the highest praise Cal could give me. I was so pleased I even forgot about Eve for two minutes. Then I checked the clock. 9.30 pm.

Where was she?

What was she doing?

It started obsessing me. I couldn't concentrate any more. By 9.45 I was practically screaming with frustration and Cal was starting to giving me odd looks, like I was some kind of psycho.

And then Eve and George walked in.

He had his arm round her shoulders. That was the first thing I noticed. Then that Eve was wearing clothes I hadn't seen before. A long, fitted coat that looked really expensive. He must've bought it for her. *Jesus*.

He was buying her away from me.

# 16

# An apology

Eve's face went red.

Jealousy surged through me, making me feel sick to my stomach.

George slid his hand off Eve's back. He started talking at me, too fast, trying to smooth everything over.

I just stared at Eve.

'Fancy a beer, Cal?' George said, edging towards the kitchen.

I propped the guitar against the sofa and walked silently to the front door.

'Luke?' Eve smiled at me and my jealousy twisted into this huge miserable knot in my stomach. 'D'you want to go for a walk?'

I nodded and stood back to let her leave. I didn't look round or say goodbye to the others.

I followed Eve down the stairs and out onto the pavement. It was cold and clear, the sky a deep, dark, blue.

'Nice coat,' I said, drily.

Eve nodded. 'It's another one of George's sister's things. He gave it to me before we left Cornwall. He's lent me a mobile too.'

'How thoughtful of him,' I said.

Eve frowned at me. 'Luke? For God's sake. You don't . . .?'

I raised my eyes.

'Luke, he's not . . . We're not . . .'

'No?'

'No. I *asked* Cal to call you up and get you round. And I *asked* George if we could go out for a couple of hours while I got up the courage to come back and talk to you.'

'You're not with George?' I tried to slide this slice of information into the melting pot of jealousy and misery that was my brain.

'No.' Eve shook her head impatiently. 'Well. I nearly let him kiss me once. I was so upset and he was being so nice. But I didn't . . . I couldn't . . .' She turned and stared at me. I said nothing. I was completely focused on pushing the image of George trying to kiss Eve out of my head.

'It drives me mad how possessive guys are,' she said. 'All those "are you up for it" looks I get. I used to think they were about me – about people being interested in

159

*me* – but they're not. All those looks mean is: "Can I own your body tonight?", "Can I hire your body out tonight?". And then, the least little thing and you get jealous. For nothing.'

I clenched my jaw. 'That's good, coming from someone who's jealous of something that meant absolutely nothing to me.'

'OK, OK.' Eve sighed, as we walked along the pavement. 'I don't want to fight. I'm not mad at you about that . . . not really. I mean, I hate thinking about it, about you wanting someone else, but I understand how it happened . . . and you were right, you didn't know when I was coming back. And I can even see now why you didn't want to tell me. It's just . . .'

'What?' I said.

'When I was in Mallorca that first week at the convent and Mum had totally freaked out and Dad was acting like this paranoid monster, I sort of collapsed in on myself. I felt so stupid – like somehow I should have fought harder against what my dad was doing. I'm nearly seventeen. I shouldn't be letting them tell me what to do like this. I felt so alone and helpless. And all that kept me going was you.'

She stopped and stroked my face with her hands. I closed my eyes, my anger and jealousy melting away. All I could feel was how amazing being with her was. How natural. How heart-breakingly, lust-inducingly, soul-achingly right.

'In my head I turned you into this perfect hero who was going to save me from my life,' Eve said. Her voice sounded tight and strained, like she was close to tears. 'I didn't realise until last week but that's why I could never draw you properly. Because I wasn't seeing you. I was seeing this romantic image of who I wanted you to be. Like something from a fairy tale or a movie.'

I opened my eyes. She was talking fast now, gulping back sobs.

'When I saw you that first night . . . you looked so gorgeous and I wanted to be with you so much. And I let myself believe that the image I had of you was real.' Her voice cracked. 'Because . . . because you came with me. You gave up everything to come with me.' She gazed up at me, her eyes shining wet in the streetlight.

'And I'd come with you again.' My voice was a whisper. I lent my forehead down onto hers. 'I couldn't love you more than I do.'

'I know, but . . . but . . . When I found out about you sleeping with that girl and not telling me, I realised that you weren't this perfect guy. I mean I *really* realised it. And it hurt so much. It made me feel so alone. Like I couldn't trust you or *anyone*.'

Tears were running down her cheeks. I wiped them away, feeling like crying myself. 'Eve,' I said. 'Please . . .'

'I don't want to be hurt any more,' she said. 'I'm scared. I don't want to risk being hurt.' She turned to go back towards George's flat.

I grabbed her arm. I had no idea what to say. I just knew I couldn't let her go.

'That's stupid.' I pulled her round to face me. 'I mean, OK, so your mum let you down because she was scared of your dad and your dad locked you up because he was scared of you growing up. But . . . but if you get scared too – about being with me, just because I made one mistake – then no one wins and nothing good comes out of it.'

Eve stared at me.

And I suddenly knew there was nothing I could do or say that would make her less scared. I had to let her work it out for herself. I took a deep breath.

'I'm going to go now,' I said. 'So just think about it. And don't go back to Cornwall. Go and see your mum. Call your dad. You're right. You can't let them tell you what to do any more. You want to go to art college. I know you do. I know you should. But it can't happen if you keep running away from everything. You have to tell them how you feel and what you want. I'll help if you like.' I squeezed her hand. 'I'm going to come round to George's flat on

Saturday night. And pick you up. And we're going to go out. OK? So . . . so if you don't care about me you can tell me then and I'll leave you alone, but if you do care, then . . . then . . .'

But my throat was too choked for me to finish my sentence. So I leaned forwards, kissed her forehead and walked away.

All the way home I thought of things I should have said. Like how much I loved her and how much I'd missed her. That's what she would have wanted to hear. Not how I thought she wasn't perfect. Not a pigging lecture on how she should call her mum and dad. I hadn't even mentioned that Jonno had spoken to me. Which meant what I said about her parents probably hadn't made sense. And I hadn't told her about Matt leaving Mum or how sick she was. *Stupid. Stupid.* At least then Eve would have felt sorry for me.

'I totally cocked it up,' I said to Ryan in the cafeteria at school the next day. 'I said all this rubbish that made sense at the time, but they were all the wrong things.'

'Like what?' he said, grabbing a bag of crisps off the counter.

I repeated the gist of what I'd said. As I spoke I watched

Ryan's mouth fall open. *God.* It must have been worse than I thought.

I dried up. *You tosser, Luke. You total idiot.*

'Go on, then,' I said bitterly. 'Tell me where I went wrong.'

Ryan closed his mouth. 'Actually, I was thinking how I'd never heard you say anything half so intelligent before.'

I shrugged and followed him over to the sandwich trays. What did Ryan know? But a glimmer of hope began to shine through the darkness in my head.

He grinned as he picked out a ham-and-cheese sarnie. 'I'm going to this party on Saturday night. Why don't you come, and bring Eve?'

I frowned. 'I'd thought it would be better if we were on our own.'

Ryan laughed. 'So where you gonna take her, then? You haven't got any money. It's freezing outside. Which just leaves your place. That'll be nice with your mum and her friend listening in.'

He was right. Going out anywhere on a Saturday night without any money was impossible. And I was totally broke. I hadn't realised how easy George's money had made everything. I couldn't ask Mum for any either. Her maternity pay from work only just covered our bills. And Matt hadn't sent her anything since he'd left.

'I'll even bring your share of the booze,' Ryan said lazily, handing me the tuna mayonnaise sandwich I was reaching for.

'Thanks, Ry,' I said, an idea forming in my head. 'Just for that I'll bring you a present. Something that doesn't cost any money.'

'Oh yeah?' he said. 'What?'

But I refused to say.

# 17

# Matt the prat

On Saturday morning Trisha moved out. I helped her pack up her car and unload it at the other end. She was really big now – and every time she talked her breath sounded wheezy.

'Are you sure you'll be all right?' I said. 'Call me if you need any help, won't you? I can look after Alice anytime. Well, most times.'

'Thanks, Luke.' Trisha smiled at me. 'You know I'm really proud of you – looking after your mum and everything.'

I blushed. Somehow praise from Trisha wasn't patronising like it was from most adults. She reached up and ruffled my hair. 'That girlfriend of yours doesn't know what she's missing.'

I scarpered out of the house before my face got so hot it set the place on fire.

*

I knew something was wrong as soon as I opened the front door at home. For a second I sensed the tension in the air. And then I heard Mum sobbing.

'No word. No money. And now you turn up out of the blue and all you want is your stuff? What about Sam?'

I strode into the living room. Mum was on the sofa, her head in her hands.

Matt was towering over her, red-faced and furious. 'Don't guilt-trip me about this,' he yelled. 'I'm not Simon. He *wanted* kids. He *wanted* to settle down. Not me. *Never.*'

'Please stop shouting,' Mum wept. She saw me by the door and sat up. 'Luke.'

But my eyes were fixed on Matt, a deep hatred coursing through me. How dare he yell at Mum like that? How dare he act like having a son was something he could take or leave? And . . .

'How *dare* you say his name.'

'Luke.' Mum's voice was a low warning.

Matt turned towards me. He frowned, not understanding.

I marched over, my fists clenched. 'My dad's name. How dare you come here and talk about him. He'd be ashamed he ever thought you were his friend.'

Matt curled his lip. 'Get out of here.'

The rage in my head boiled over. This was my home.
*Mine.*

I punched – all my hate in my fist. He ducked. Caught my arm. Tried to push me away. I pushed back. I could take him. I knew I could. He was only a little taller than me. And I was just as strong. Stronger.

'YOU BASTARD!' This massive roar ripped out of my mouth.

I guess I must have looked scary as hell because Matt let go and took a step away from me.

Mum was still on the sofa, her mouth moving but no sound coming out.

I'd never felt so powerful. So sure of my own power.

I shoved Matt. He stumbled backwards.

'STOP BULLYING HER,' I yelled, my chest heaving. Almost choking on the words.

Matt stared at me. For a second I thought he was going to try and hit me after all. Then he lowered his eyes and started walking to the door. 'I'm just getting my stuff,' he muttered.

I sat down next to Mum, my whole body shaking. She was trembling too, so I put my arm round her. We sat there in silence while Matt stomped round the house, gathering up his belongings.

In my heart I was glad he was going for good. Glad he

wouldn't be around any more to stick his nose in our business, and make Mum miserable. And then I thought about baby Sam and felt guilty. Not having a dad sucked.

Sam deserved one. Even one as rubbish as Matt.

I got up and went to find him.

He was in Mum's bedroom, taking some shirts out of the wardrobe. He looked up warily, clearly taking a second to check I wasn't about to swing another punch at him, then went back to work. I leaned my head against the wall.

'You can't just leave,' I said. 'Mum's ill. And what are we supposed to tell Sam when he asks where his dad is?'

Matt glared at me. 'You don't know anything about it.'

'About what?' I raised my eyebrows. 'Responsibility? Parenting? Or being a total arsehole?'

Matt tore a shirt off its hanger. 'I'm forty-five,' he muttered. 'That probably sounds really old to you. But it isn't. I've got masses of stuff I still want to do. I can't get sucked into all this domestic crap.' He looked round at me and sighed. 'Me and your mum were never going to last,' he said. 'She was always your dad's girl. I was with Simon when he met her for the first time. You've never seen two people fall in love faster. Or make it last better.'

I stared at him. I'd never really thought about Dad dying from anyone else's point of view before. I suddenly realised – for the first time – what *Mum* had actually lost when he died.

Matt shook his head. 'She doesn't love me. I was just there at the right time for a while.'

He shoved the shirts he had taken from the wardrobe into a bag and walked to the door.

'What about Sam?'

Matt paused, leaning on the door frame. 'I'll send some money for him. I'll set something up. Maybe in a few years . . . Look, I know I look bad to you right now, but Sam'll be better off not knowing me at all than having me waltz in and out of his life whenever I feel like it.' He smiled. 'Anyway, Sam's got you, now.'

*What?* I opened my mouth, determined to make him see how ridiculous that was. But Matt was already padding down the stairs. I heard him talking quietly to Mum and then the front door clicking shut.

I wandered back into the living room. To my surprise Mum wasn't crying any more. In fact her eyes looked clearer than I'd seen them since I got back from Cornwall.

'It's OK,' she said. 'Really. It'll be OK.'

Sam started crying upstairs and she got up. As she passed me in the doorway she stopped. 'Your dad would be proud of you.'

I shrugged, feeling embarrassed and pleased all at once. 'I can stay in tonight if you want, Mum.'

She kissed my cheek. 'No, sweetheart, you go out and have some fun with your friends. The baby and I are going to be just fine.'

She went upstairs.

I stared out of the window, suddenly feeling very, very old.

I got ready really carefully that night. My heart was thumping as I rang on the doorbell of George's flat. To my surprise, Alejandro opened the door. He beamed at me. 'Hey, Luke.'

'Hi,' I said. Eve appeared next to him.

'Hi.' She smiled shyly at me. 'Alejandro just showed up. He's only here one more evening. I said he could come to the party. Is that all right?'

'Oh.' I struggled not to feel this meant she was trying to avoid talking to me – and failed.

Alejandro's smile morphed into a look of concern. 'If me coming is a problem, it's OK. But later I'm going to a club to meet friends, so the party is just for an hour or two to see you and Eva. Tomorrow I am going back to Spain. Another tour.'

I tried to smile at him. 'Course it's OK,' I lied. ''S good to see you.'

I quickly guessed that Alejandro had no idea what was going on between me and Eve. He had obviously assumed we were back together. Trust Eve. She knew he would have given us space if he'd known and she didn't want to leave him on his own.

Cal and George were packing up their stuff, arguing loudly in the background. Eve whispered to me that Jess had started seeing some guy she'd met at George's party and that Cal had decided to stay on in London. 'It's the end of the band,' she said.

'Really?' I wondered whether Cal was going to set up a new group. Whether, maybe, he'd consider letting me join.

'Yeah.' Eve sighed. 'George is going back to Cornwall on Monday.'

I forgot about Cal and the guitar for a moment. If George was going back to Cornwall, would Eve go with him?

I couldn't work her out. She looked unbearably sexy in this low-cut, glittery top and old jeans. But she was avoiding my eyes. We walked next to each other up to the tube station. I told her about her dad's call last week, apologising for not having mentioned it before. I thought she might be cross, but she didn't react at all. She tried to give me back my iPod, but I told her to keep it. Then she asked about Mum and I told her what had happened with Matt earlier.

She sighed. 'God, your poor mum,' she said, looking at me properly for the first time.

I stared at her, drinking up her face, suddenly desperate to know where I stood. 'Eve . . .?'

She put her hand on my arm. 'Let's talk when we get there. OK?'

What did that mean? That she wanted other people around when she dumped me for good?

# 18

# Back to the start

The party was being held in a tiny, second-floor flat, a few miles east of the City. As soon as we arrived, I knew we weren't exactly in for the night of the century. Not enough people, hardly any booze and some rubbish music blaring out from a pair of tinny speakers.

Ryan was there when Eve, Alejandro and I arrived. He hugged Eve and clapped me and Alejandro heavily on the back. He was already a little bit drunk. I frowned. The last few times I'd gone out with Ryan he'd got drunk really early on in the evening. Why was he doing that?

'So where's my free gift?' he grinned at me.

'I didn't say it was a free gift.' I watched him pull a half-bottle of vodka out of his trouser pocket and take a swig. 'I said a present that didn't cost any money. It'll be here any minute. Hey, Ry.' I grabbed the bottle as he swung it up to his mouth for a second time. 'Why are you drinking like this? It's stupid getting pissed before anything's even happened.'

Ryan scowled as he wrenched the vodka out of my hands. 'Numbs the pain, man,' he said bitterly. He put the bottle to his lips, then did a double take. I followed his gaze and saw Chloe in the doorway.

'There. Your present's arrived.' I said, relieved that Ryan was still relatively sober, but massively regretting that I'd thought it was a good idea to tell Chloe he'd said he wanted her to come to the party. OK, so they'd both more or less admitted they really missed each other. But it wasn't any of my business. And Chloe was going to freak when she realised I'd lied to her. Which was going to happen in about five seconds flat unless Ryan showed some interest in her being here.

Chloe was still at the door. She hadn't noticed us yet.

Ryan watched her shuck off her jacket. 'That's my present?' He snorted, then screwed the top back on his vodka bottle and shoved it in his pocket. 'Thought you said it didn't cost any money. Chloe's frigging high maintenance, man.'

My heart sank. Chloe was now looking round the room. Some guy I was sure she didn't know swaggered over to her.

Why was Ryan waiting?

'Go on, then.' I prodded him in the back. 'What you gonna do about *her*?'

That was our in-joke, pre-pulling line from months and months ago.

I wasn't certain Ryan had even heard me. He was still staring intently at Chloe. At last, he walked forwards towards her.

I breathed a sigh of relief. At least he wanted to talk. I turned round. Alejandro was wandering across the living room to the MP3 player connected to the speakers. I could see girls checking him out as he passed. Eve touched my arm and smiled. 'That was a nice thing, getting Chlo and Ry together,' she said.

I shrugged. 'Someone should be happy,' I said glumly.

Alejandro had reached the MP3 player. He chatted to the girl standing next to it. Even at this distance I could see she was practically melting in front of him. He was pointing to a song. The girl nodded.

'Luke?' Eve paused. I held my breath waiting for her to go on.

And then two things happened in quick succession. A new song blasted into the party. A brilliant dancey rock track that I knew Alejandro loved.

Three seconds later, the air filled with this piercing screech.

I spun round. Chloe and Ryan were standing about half a metre apart from each other, both completely red in the face.

'YOU PIGGING LIAR, RY.'

'YOU'RE THE LIAR.'

'I KNOW OF ABOUT TEN GIRLS AT LEAST.'

'OH YEAH? WHAT ABOUT ALL THAT CRAP YOU GAVE ME ABOUT NEEDING SPACE?'

'HOW DARE YOU LIE TO ME, RYAN.'

'YOU JUST WANTED TO SCREW OTHER GUYS. WHICH, BY THE WAY, IS ABSOLUTELY FINE WITH ME.'

I stared, along with most of the rest of the people in the room, as they carried on shouting at each other. Someone turned the music up, but Ryan and Chloe didn't appear to notice.

I turned away, my head in my hands. 'Oh God,' I moaned.

Alejandro had reappeared next to Eve. He grinned at me. 'No worries. You have provided the free party entertainment.'

It was true. Everyone in the room, even the ones still dancing, were watching Ryan and Chloe. They were now hurling long links of swear words at each other.

Eve shook her head. 'I've never got how can they do that in public.' She glanced at me then looked back at Ry and Chloe.

'I HATE YOU.'

'I HATE YOU WORSE, YOU BASTARD.'

I studied Eve's face, wondering if she was thinking that if she and I had done more shouting in public we might not be here, now.

Wherever that was.

I was suddenly aware that the shouting had stopped. Eve was still staring, wide-eyed, at where I knew Ryan and Chloe were standing behind me.

I turned round.

They were kissing. No. They were devouring each other. How had they gone, in seconds, from all that anger to this – their mouths locked, with not a fraction of a centimetre separating their bodies? The people standing and dancing near them started applauding and whistling. Ryan and Chloe appeared as entirely oblivious as they had done earlier.

I turned away, embarrassed at seeing Chloe in such a massive snog. Then I looked over at Eve and felt embarrassed that we were so far away from one ourselves.

'Wow.' She was still watching them. Alejandro had vanished again.

'If you can tear yourself away from the live sex show,' I muttered, 'perhaps we can talk.'

She grinned across at me. Then she saw how unsmiling I was and the grin slid from her face.

We went into the hallway outside the flat where it was a bit quieter. We sat down with our backs against the wall. The couple opposite us were all over each other. I looked down at the floor.

A long pause. The music in the living room changed – to another rock track I knew Alejandro liked.

'I thought about what you said,' Eve began, tentatively. 'And I realised that my mum and dad *are* scared. You were right. They're scared and they're making the wrong choices and I shouldn't run away from the situation any more. I should stand up to them.'

I looked up at her.

'But thinking all that,' Eve stammered, 'just made *me* feel more scared than ever.'

*Oh.* That didn't sound hopeful.

Another long pause.

Eve sat back and gazed thoughtfully at the couple opposite us. The boy was kissing the girl so eagerly he was almost pinning her against the wall. Her hands were pressed flat on the ground beside her and her eyes were open. She didn't look at all comfortable.

*Ease up, mate,* I thought. *Or you'll be toast.*

'Would you come with me if I went to see my mum tomorrow?' she said.

'Sure.' *What about us, Eve? What about us?*

She looked at me. 'Would you come, even if we're not going out any more?'

*Oh Christ.* 'Course.' I shrugged. 'I told you I wanted to help.'

Eve moved the tiniest bit closer to me.

'And would you mind if I said we could never, ever have sex?'

*Yes. Obviously.*

'Mmmn,' I said, slowly. 'I would mind because it's hard to stop when I want you so much. But I don't mind waiting until you're ready. Just so long as I know that you're waiting because *it's* not right. Not because *I'm* not right.'

She grinned. 'You're really listening to me, aren't you?'

I shrugged. Eve moved even closer. Her face was nearly touching mine.

'You didn't used to listen, you know,' she said. 'I mean you tried sometimes, especially at first. And you did it more than anyone else I'd ever been out with – but now it feels different. Like you know me better . . . like . . .'

'Like we're friends, too?' I said.

She nodded, her nose brushing the end of mine. 'Exactly.'

We stayed there, staring at each other for a moment.

'What are you thinking?' she said.

I could feel my face relaxing into a smile.

'I'm thinking,' I murmured, 'how I'd really, really like you to stop talking now and kiss me.'

I've got no idea how long we sat there, our arms wrapped round each other. Alejandro came over to say goodbye – that he was going to his club. He appeared to be with some boy he'd met at the party. Tall, with spiky blond hair. The boy kept glancing over at Alejandro with big, sexed-up eyes, as if he couldn't believe his luck. But he didn't say anything and Alejandro didn't introduce him. He stood to one side as Alejandro said goodbye to me, then gave Eve a big hug.

We sat down against the wall again and watched them weave their way to the stairs to the ground floor. Eve sighed. 'Why is it all the really good-looking guys are gay?'

'Hey,' I said, prodding her in the ribs.

She laughed, her eyes pulling me in again. But just as I leaned towards her, Ryan and Chloe walked over.

'Eve,' Chloe squealed.

'Chloe.'

As they flung their arms round each other, Ryan put his hand on my shoulder. 'Can I have a word?' He looked serious.

'Sure.' I let him lead me a metre or so away down the

corridor from Eve and Chloe. 'So you two back together?'
I said.

'Looks like it.' Ryan's face split into a lopsided grin. 'I
knew she wouldn't be able to stay away from me for long.'

I rolled my eyes, but before I could say anything sar-
castic, Ryan's face went serious again. 'Listen, man,' he
said. 'Hayley's here.'

'*What?*'

My stomach gave a sick lurch. I peered towards the flat.
The front door was several metres away and the room
beyond too dark to make out individual faces. 'Is she in
that room with the music?'

'Yeah. She turned up about half an hour ago. Walked
right past you apparently. You didn't even notice her. She's
getting really tanked up now and punchy with it. She came
over. Had a go at me about you being an arsehole for not
calling her. Like it was *my* fault.' Ryan shook his head in
disbelief. 'Course Chlo was really rude to her. She was
dead funny actually. Suggested that Hayley might like it if
she speed-dialled her number to every guy in the room.
God, Chloe's amazing. She just gets this look in her eye
sometimes, like a missile locking on its target and you
know that she's going to give—'

'Ry,' I snapped. 'What about Hayley?'

'Oh yeah.' Ryan frowned. 'I thought you should know

she was here. 'Cause I think if she has much more to drink she might come over and have a go at you, too.' He glanced over at where Eve and Chloe were still talking.

I could see what he was thinking. No way did I want Hayley and Eve to meet. That could ruin *everything*.

'Thanks, Ry.' I turned away. I had to get Eve to leave straight away.

He punched my arm and nodded towards Chloe. 'Er . . . and thanks too . . . er,' he said. 'For . . . you know . . .'

'No problem.' I grinned at him. 'I mean, who else'd go out with her?'

I hurried over to Eve, slipped my arm round her waist and whispered in her ear that we should go. She frowned at me.

'But I'm having a good time,' she said. 'I haven't seen Chlo for ages.'

I stared at Chloe helplessly.

'I'll come round tomorrow,' Chloe said quickly. 'To ours, I mean. Maybe we could meet there.'

Eve's frown deepened. 'What's going on?' she said.

'Nothing,' I said. 'It's just . . .'

I stopped, catching sight of Hayley in the doorway of the living room. Her hair was redder and wilder than I'd remembered. She was wearing a skin-tight dress and her

183

wrists and fingers were loaded down with jewellery. She stared at me, her eyes hard and slightly unfocused.

Her mouth curled into an ugly sneer. She was going to come over. She was going to talk to me.

*Shit.*

# 19

# The fight

I tore my eyes away from Hayley.

'Come *on,* Eve,' I said, forcing a smile. 'Maybe we should try and find Alejandro's club.'

She shook her head. 'It's a *gay* club, Luke. You'd hate—'

'OK, I've gotta pee,' Chloe said urgently. 'Come with me to the bathroom, Eve. We can talk there.'

She dragged Eve into the flat. Hayley glared at them as they passed. I prayed Eve hadn't noticed.

Hayley turned round. She stared at me again, then started walking slowly over. Ryan prodded me in the back.

'What you gonna do about *her,* man?' he said drily.

*Oh crap.*

'Hey. Luke.' Hayley's voice was an icy, slurred drawl. 'How *are* you?'

'OK.'

Hayley narrowed her eyes accusingly.

185

There was a long, tense silence. Rock music and excited chatter filled the air around us.

'I'm sorry . . .' I stammered. 'I mean . . . I'm sorry I haven't been in touch. That I . . . er . . . I . . . didn't . . . er . . .'

'That you didn't call me after you screwed me in my sister's boyfriend's flat? After you left before I was even awake?' She sounded cold and ironic. I had no idea whether she was really upset about it, or just taking the piss out of me.

I decided to play it straight.

'Yeah. Look. I guess it was mean just to run off. So I am sorry. But . . . but I didn't actually *say* I'd call you, did I?'

Hayley shook her head. 'No, you're right, Luke,' she said, slowly. 'You didn't say you'd call. And, to be honest, I didn't really want you to. It wasn't that great. For *me*.'

I nodded. 'OK.' *Really? Was I that bad?* 'OK, well. OK. Thanks. So . . . We're OK, then?' I backed away.

'Yeah, everything's fine,' Hayley slurred. 'So long as you're absolutely, definitely sorry.'

I stared at her, wondering what the hell was going on inside her head.

'OK,' I said, again.

'Hey.' Hayley sneered. 'You owe me a beer.'

My mind flashed back to the party in December and how she'd leaned against the counter in that club, buying me a drink.

'Right. Course.' I beckoned Ryan over. 'Hey, Ry,' I said. 'Any of our stash left? Hayley wants a beer.'

Ryan shot me an 'Are you mad?' look, and vanished inside the flat. I stood there, awkwardly, hoping he'd come back quickly. I tried to work out how long Chloe and Eve had been gone.

'Er . . . d'you mind if we don't hang out to drink it? The beer, I mean.'

Hayley raised her eyebrows.

'It's just, my girlfriend . . .' I said. 'I don't think she'd . . . er . . . maybe it's best if we don't . . . er . . . if she doesn't see us talking . . .'

Hayley rounded her mouth in an expression of mock surprise. '*Really*?' she said, with heavy emphasis.

*Man, I'm drowning here. Where the hell are you, Ryan?*

At that moment he reappeared with two bottles of beer. He handed one to Hayley and took a swig out of the other himself. The music from the party changed to a new track with a pounding bass.

'Where's mine?' I said.

He patted his pocket. 'You can have the vodka,' he whispered. 'You're gonna need it.'

'Luke and I were just talking about how things ended between us,' Hayley slurred.

*No, we weren't. We didn't have 'things'. We had a shag. Why won't you just go away?*

And then, suddenly, Eve and Chloe were back. Eve wound her arm round my waist. I was standing between her and Hayley.

I shot an imploring look at Ryan. *Get me out of here.*

Eve smiled at Hayley. She glared back and swigged at her beer. I stared at the carpet in front of me. An empty beer bottle lay on its side beside Chloe's feet. I could feel Eve leaning against me on one side and sensed Hayley on the other, standing too close, breathing heavily.

I tried to work out how on earth I could convince Eve we needed to leave. Right now. And then she smiled at Hayley again.

'So, how d'you know Ryan and Luke?' she asked politely.

Ryan spluttered his beer over the carpet.

I closed my eyes.

*Too late.*

'Well,' Hayley slurred. 'I knew Ryan first.' She paused. 'But I know Luke better. If you know what I mean?'

There was a horrible silence. Just the party music pumping out behind us. I could feel Eve stiffen beside me. I opened my eyes.

'Oh,' Hayley said, pretending to be all shocked again. 'You must be Luke's *girlfriend*. The one he doesn't want seeing us drinking together.'

'Hayley.' I could hear every ounce of Ryan's charm in his voice. 'Come *on*. Don't do this.'

'Do what?' Hayley smiled nastily. 'I don't think it's got anything to do with you. Though you obviously know all the details. Still, I suppose Luke had to boast to *somebody*.'

Another horrible silence. I desperately wanted to grab Eve and move away, but my feet seemed to be glued to the floor.

I forced myself to look right at Hayley, pleading with her to stop.

Her eyes were like tiny stones.

'So this is nice, isn't it?' she snarled at me. 'You and Ryan, both being here. With your ugly bitch girlfriends.'

'Hey.' Ryan, Chloe and I all shouted at once. Eve gasped. My heart pounded.

'Hayleeee.' One of Hayley's friends rushed over and tried to tug her away. 'Hay. Come on. Let's go.'

'Yeah. Go, you stupid cow,' Chloe spat, kicking at the empty beer bottle on the floor. It knocked against Hayley's feet. 'You're just embarrassing yourself.'

Hayley swore. She lashed out at Chloe, her long red nails flashing like claws in the dim corridor light.

Chloe jumped sideways. She bumped into Eve, avoiding Hayley's fingers by millimetres. With a roar Hayley lashed out again, but this time her fist was clenched. It missed Chloe completely and smacked, hard, against Eve's face.

Time seemed to stop for a second. Then Eve's hand flew to her cheek. Her eyes widened as she stared at Hayley.

A black fury filled me. Even worse than when I'd seen Matt shouting at Mum. Almost without being aware of what I was doing, I reached out and grabbed Hayley's arms. 'THAT'S ENOUGH.' I could hear it was my voice, yelling, but it seemed to be coming from somewhere far outside my head.

Hayley glared up at me, trying to wrench her arms away. 'GET OFF ME,' she shouted.

'Stop it then,' I said, gripping her arms more tightly.

I could feel Hayley tense every muscle. 'YOU WERE CRAP,' she shouted. 'You were rubbish. I just . . .' She stopped suddenly, her arms still raised against mine. Her eyes flickered sideways, to where I knew Eve was standing, then back to me. She gazed at our arms entwined, at my whole body . . . up and down. 'This remind you of anything, Luke?' She threw me a sly smile.

And with a flourish she turned away and flounced off.

# 20

# Facing facts

I stared across at Eve. Her face was white, except for a red mark across one cheekbone, where Hayley had hit her. Her eyes were blank. She pressed her lips together. I couldn't tell whether she was angry, or just trying not to cry.

Hayley's friend was bobbing up and down beside me. In spite of the horrified sounds she was making, it was obvious she was enjoying all the drama.

'Oh my God,' she said. 'I can't *believe* she did that. I didn't realise she was that *bothered*. You must have *really* upset her when you slept with her. I mean—'

'P'raps you'd better see if she's all right, then,' I snapped.

*Jesus.*

I reached out and took Eve's arm. 'Let's go,' I said. I dragged her past Chloe and Ryan, and down the stairs to the ground floor.

We stumbled out of the apartment building and into the

clear, cold night air. I stood there for a few seconds, taking deep breaths, feeling the world fall back into place.

Then I turned to Eve. I stared at the red mark on her cheek. The skin was broken where one of Hayley's rings must have caught it. 'Are you OK?' I said. 'I'm so, so sorry that happened.'

'That was her, then,' Eve said, dully.

'Please don't let this change anything. I—'

'Did you really tell Ryan what you'd done?' Eve said. 'You know, boasting, like she said?'

My mind flashed back to how impressed Ryan had been when I'd told him about Hayley. How much I'd enjoyed telling him.

'He sort of guessed,' I said, not meeting her eyes.

*God.* I was coming out of this looking like a total arsehole.

Maybe I was one.

'It was just one time.' I shoved my hands in my pockets and stared at the pavement. 'And I know you don't understand this, but it wasn't special. It was just . . . just what it was.'

I looked up. Eve shivered. I wanted to put my arms round her, but she seemed so distant, so wrapped up in her own thoughts, I didn't dare.

'I left my bag up there,' Eve said, pointing up at the flat.

'It's got my – George's – phone in it. Would you go back and get it?'

I nodded, but didn't move. 'Is your face all right?'

*Will you still be here when I get back?*

'I'm fine.' Eve sounded strangely calm. 'I just want the phone.'

I raced up the stairs and back into the party. There was no sign of Hayley. Ryan and Chloe were deep in conversation where I'd left them. I rushed over and reached behind the corner table where I'd seen Eve stash her bag. I retrieved it and stood up.

Ryan was grinning at me. 'That was wild,' he said. He lowered his voice so Chloe couldn't hear him. 'Was it me or was it massively horny when Hayley started that cat fight?'

I stared at him. 'You are *twisted,* mate.'

Ryan's grin deepened. I thought of Eve waiting outside and tore back downstairs, leaping down the steps three at a time.

She was still there. I gave her the little handbag, my heart beating fast. 'Eve?'

She looked at me. 'It wasn't as bad as I thought. Seeing her, I mean. Really. In some ways it's easier now I know what she looks like.' She paused. 'Though she has got a great body.'

'Has she?' I said. 'I didn't notice.'

'Yeah, right.' Eve rolled her eyes. 'Anyway, that's not the point. The point is that seeing her and knowing what you did . . . it didn't make me go back to feeling bad about myself. I'm not the one who did anything wrong. Why should I feel worthless? That's why I want the phone. I decided. I'm gonna call my dad right now.'

'You sure?' I glanced at my own phone. It was well after midnight.

'He'll be up,' she said. 'Spanish hours. Remember? Will you wait while I call him?'

I nodded. We walked down the street while she dialled the number. Her hands shook as she held the mobile up to her ear. It struck me how brave she was being confronting her dad like this. I reached out and wrapped my arms round her.

She didn't pull away.

I could hear the phone on the other end ringing. Then Jonno's voice, barking out a hello. I leaned against the wall behind us, letting Eve rest against me. She was totally calm and strong as she talked to him. She explained how she wanted to go back to school for the rest of the year, then take a foundation course and go to art college.

'I've sorted it all out, Dad,' she said. 'So you have to accept it.'

Jonno was upset and angry at first, accusing her of being

thoughtless and selfish. But then he calmed down a little. I could hear him talking more softly, asking if she was all right, agreeing to fly over so they could talk.

And then Eve said she wanted to live at home with her mum again.

*Yes.*

My heart soared. I squeezed her waist. She felt amazing. I slipped my hand under her jacket and kissed her neck.

Eve pushed me away, grinning. She talked to her dad for about a minute longer, then flicked the phone shut and turned back to me.

'He's getting on a plane.' She beamed at me. 'I'm gonna see him at Mum's tomorrow. Oh Luke, everything's going to be all right now. I'm going to *make* it all right.'

She hugged me. 'Can I come back to yours?' she asked. 'It's just George's flat'll be full of people smoking dope until four am. Anyway, I'm going to see Mum tomorrow and you're much closer.'

'Course,' I grinned.

We walked down to the bus stop and got two night-buses back to my house. Everything felt different. Maybe it was the fact that all the crap we'd been through felt like it was almost over, but there was a freedom in how we were. Like we were totally ourselves now. Totally comfortable with each other.

We talked all the way home on the crowded bus, Eve full of her plans for her artwork. I told her how playing the guitar felt. How much I loved it. How I wanted to carry on playing with Cal, but had no money to buy an instrument or pay for lessons.

'It's the only thing I've ever done that I really loved,' I said. 'The only thing I could imagine doing for ever.'

We got off the bus, walked up the high street and turned off in the direction of my house. We didn't stop talking until we reached the corner. Then Eve stood still, facing me, holding my hand.

'I was thinking about that girl – Hayley,' she said. 'It's weird.'

'Oh?' I said, feeling nervous.

Eve moved closer to me. 'She was really upset, you know. That's why she was so horrible.'

I looked away. 'I know,' I said.

'D'you know what it made me think?' Eve said.

*That I'm an arsehole.*

*That you're worth ten times more than I can ever give you.*

*That you don't love me any more.*

I shook my head.

'Well.' Eve moved even closer. 'It made me think that I could afford to feel sorry for her. D'you know why?'

I looked at her and shook my head again.

'Because I got you,' Eve smiled. 'And she didn't.'

We stared at each other for a second. And then we kissed.

It wasn't like any other kiss.

It was everything. All the friendship. All the lust. All the love.

All in one kiss.

It was so sweet and deep and then so overwhelming, so blindingly hot that I could hardly walk when Eve took my hand again and tugged me towards the house.

As we walked along the path to the front door Eve fell silent.

Inside, there was a note on the floor by the front door: *Trisha is having her baby. I've gone round to look after Alice. See you later. Be good. Love Mum.*

I picked up the note and glanced at Eve. 'Empty house.' I raised an eyebrow.

She nodded and slipped off her coat.

*Jesus.* Everything about her turned me on. Even tiny things: the way her top lip dipped into a V in the middle; that slightly shy expression in her eyes; the creamy skin rounding over her shoulder.

'What do you want to do?' I croaked.

*Because I want you so much I can hardly stand it.*

Eve said nothing.

'It's just that I'd rather know,' I stammered. 'You know, whether . . . I mean it doesn't matter. That is, I mean . . . well . . .'

Eve pressed her finger against my lips. A tiny groan escaped out of my mouth. Just from that little touch.

She smiled up at me then moved closer, putting her arm round my waist. 'Maybe I should sleep in Chloe's room,' she said.

I stared at her, all confused by the difference between what she was saying and how she was looking at me. *God. The way she was looking at me.*

'What?' I was practically on my knees now. 'You mean on your own?'

Eve reached up and pressed her face against my cheek. 'I'm kidding,' she whispered. 'I think I might explode if we don't do it right now.'

# 21

# Hiding

We ran upstairs to my bedroom.

As I led Eve past Mum's room I considered going in there and using the bigger bed. But only for a few seconds. It was just too weird, thinking about being in Mum's bed.

Inside my own room I dropped Eve's hand and darted over to my wardrobe. I grabbed the packet of condoms I'd stashed in there months ago. Then I straightened up and looked round at all the mess: all the old posters and the music and the magazines and the clothes.

There was no stylish designer room. No four-poster double bed. No music pounding in our ears. Eve stood in front of me.

It was just her.

Just me.

Of course the first time was rubbish. Well. Rubbish for Eve. I was so off my head with wanting her that it was all over far, far too quickly. Afterwards I collapsed next to her, mumbling that I was sorry and worrying that maybe Hayley had been right about me being crap, while Eve lay there with 'Was that it?' written all over her face.

Then she told me to shut up and make her a cup of tea. And when I came back she grinned at me and drank her tea. Then she put down the mug and we started again. And this time I focused more on her – wanting it to be good for her, wanting it to be all about her.

I already knew practically every centimetre of her body. We had been going out for almost a year, after all. But this was different. Everything was different. The way she reacted when I touched her. The way she looked at me.

The way it felt.

It was getting light outside when we finally fell asleep, curled up face to face – all wrapped round each other.

My first thought was that the scrabbling sound was a mouse. I opened my eyes. Eve was gazing at me, her hair spread out on the pillow like a fan. Her cheek where Hayley had hit her was dark red, with a small cut. I stroked it, gently, still half asleep.

She smiled and I forgot the scrabbling sound and just wanted her again.

And then I heard a voice. A child's voice. Hissing an exaggerated whisper.

'Luke. Are you awake?' It was Alice.

I blinked, trying to work out what Alice was doing back in our house. She'd moved out. Yesterday. And then I remembered Trisha was having her baby and Mum was looking after Alice for her.

Which meant Mum must be here. In the house.

My eyes snapped wide open.

Eve muffled a laugh. 'Yeah, your mum's here. I just heard the front door shut.'

'Lu-uke. Open the door. Pleeese.' Alice was rattling the door handle. For one awful moment I thought she was going to walk in, and then I remembered that I'd locked the door, just before we fell asleep, exactly so that no one could do that.

I sighed with relief. 'How long have you been awake?' I murmured, knowing we should get up but not wanting to let go of her.

'Only a minute,' Eve whispered back, wriggling down a little and laying her head on my chest.'

'Lu-uu-ke.' Alice's voice was getting louder.

I stroked Eve's hair. 'Mum'll be up here in a moment,' I said. 'She'll freak when she realises the door's locked.'

'I know.' Eve sighed. 'I don't understand why I'm not panicking and running around getting dressed.'

'I know why I'm not.' I grinned. 'My brain's stopped working.'

She looked up at me with sleepy, sexy eyes. 'Stopped working or changed location?'

*Mmmn.* I leaned down to kiss her.

And then the doorbell rang.

'Who's that?' Eve wrinkled up her nose.

'Probably just the postman,' I said, running my hand down her back. 'Ignore it. When Mum comes up and knocks I'll tell her that she's just woken me up. I'll say I'm staying in bed for a bit longer. You can slip out later. No, don't . . .'

But Eve was turning away from me, reaching for her mobile. She switched it on. 'Shoot. I've got, like, ten messages.' Her whole body went rigid. 'Oh my God. It's one o'clock.'

'What?' I sat bolt upright. 'In the afternoon?'

'Yes.' Eve stared at me. 'I was supposed to be at Mum's at eleven. Dad was coming straight from the—'

'Luke.' It was Mum's voice, calling up the stairs. She sounded tense. Anxious.

My heart pounded. 'You don't think . . .?'

Footsteps sounded on the stairs. More than one set. Heavy. Tramping.

'LUKE.' It was Jonno's voice.

Eve and I stared at each other, our eyes wide. Then –
like it was choreographed – we rolled away from each
other off the bed and sprang onto the floor.

'Oh shit. Oh shit. Oh shit.' Eve scrabbled across the
carpet, retrieving her clothes. I reached down and started
pulling on my jeans.

Two sharp raps on the door. Then the handle being
twisted again.

*Oh my God.*

'Luke, are you in there?' Mum sounded really scared
now. 'Open the door.'

'Just a minute, Mum,' I shouted.

I glanced over at Eve. She was struggling to push her
legs through her jeans. I zipped mine up and looked around
for my top.

'Luke?'

Heavy blows thumped against the door.

'D'you know where Eve is?' Mum called.

'LUKE.' Jonno roared. 'Let us in or I'm breaking down
the door.'

'I'm coming,' I yelled back.

Eve was in her jeans at last, her glittery top in her hands.
'There's nowhere I can hide,' she whispered, frantically
looking round the room.

My mouth felt dry. 'You're not hiding,' I said. 'We

haven't done anything to be ashamed of. We love each other, right?'

A look of determination came over Eve's face. She nodded.

'Yes,' she said. 'We do.'

Mum and Jonno were arguing outside the door over whether or not to break it down.

'He's said he's going to open it . . .'

'Then why doesn't he? My daughter said she would meet us earlier. Something must have happened to her.'

I walked to the door.

'Wait.' Eve looked down at the glittery top. 'I can't wear this. It looks all wrong.'

'I don't think now's the time to worry about your clothes co-ordinating,' I hissed.

'No,' she whispered. 'It looks too slaggy. Like I stayed out all night.'

I shook my head. When Jonno got into this room, the last thing he was going to be worried about was what Eve was wearing.

'You're not breaking it down,' Mum shrieked.

'Eve?' It was *her* mum's voice. 'Eve, are you in there?'

Eve stared at the door. 'Shit, they're *all* here,' she whimpered. She stared back at her glittery top. 'Oh, God.'

I darted over to my wardrobe and yanked out a white shirt. I shoved it at her. 'Put this on, then.'

'EVE?' Jonno bellowed. 'Right that's it. I'm breaking down the door.'

There was a terrific thump as Jonno presumably hurled himself at the door. It wobbled and strained, but the lock held. Just.

'Stop it,' Mum yelled. 'You've got no right..'

I glanced at Eve. Her fingers were shaking as she pulled the shirt round her, trying to do up the buttons up. I realised I was still naked from the waist up.

*Hurry.*

Another massive thump. The whole house rocked as the door practically flew off its hinges. One more heave and he'd have it open.

'STOP,' I yelled. 'I'm opening the door.'

I could almost smell the tension in the corridor outside.

My hands shook as I turned the key in the lock. I pulled open the door and darted back across the room.

Jonno was first inside, storming through, head down like a bull.

I stood in front of the bed, my heart hammering in my chest. Eve was right beside me, breathing so fast she was practically hyperventilating.

Jonno stared at us, his eyes wide and furious. My mum

and Eve's mum ran in behind him, Alice dashing between their legs. 'Hiya, Luke.' She ran over and hugged my jeans.

I couldn't speak. My eyes were fixed on Jonno's face. His mouth was open. I could see him clocking Eve's bruised face and her half-buttoned shirt, then my bare chest and the sheets on the bed being all rucked up and so obviously slept in.

'Alice,' Mum said. 'Come over here. I want you to play downstairs for a bit.'

Alice obediently skipped away from me.

Jonno looked down at the carpet. I followed his gaze. *Oh God.* The condom packet was on the floor. He stared at it for a second or two, then he glanced at Eve's bruised face again.

There was this terrible pause when I could see his brain putting two and two together and making about five million.

# 22

# All about Eve

'What have you done to her?' Jonno roared. He strode across the room and shoved me backwards onto the bed. 'You evil little shit,' he yelled. 'How dare you.'

He towered over me, gripping me round the throat with both hands. He shook my neck, pressing me back into the bed. I couldn't breathe. I could hear screaming all around me but all my energy was focused on pushing him away.

I was suddenly back, reliving the night Eve's ex-boyfriend Ben had beaten me up. It wasn't the first time. I'd had a panic attack while we were in Spain. But, right now, I didn't feel scared. This time I knew what to do.

The screaming around me was getting louder. Eve and Mum were both yelling at Jonno to stop, to let me go. But there was this mad look in his eye. I know what it's like when rage fills your head like that. I was pretty sure Jonno couldn't even hear them.

I stopped trying to drag desperate slivers of air into my

lungs. And I stopped trying to pull his hands off my throat. Instead, I reached up to his face and poked him in both eyes. Really hard.

He let go of me immediately and staggered back, clutching his face. 'OWWWW.'

I sat up, massaging my neck.

Eve was immediately there, her arms round me. 'Luke, are you all right?'

Mum's face appeared over her shoulder. White and drawn. 'Luke?'

Then Jonno was back, blinking, his eyes bloodshot. 'Get away from him.'

'No.' Eve stood in front of me. Between me and her dad.

'He hurt you,' Jonno pointed to her bruised face. 'He—'

'Luke didn't do this!' Eve shouted. 'It was some drunk girl at the party we went to last night. Luke *stopped* her. OK? Leave it, Dad. Remember you promised we'd talk.'

'No way,' Jonno growled. 'Not now. Not now I see what . . . what . . . This changes everything.'

I glanced across at Eve's mum. She was shrinking back against the door. I couldn't believe it. Nothing had changed. She was going to let him take Eve away again. She was still too frightened of him to stop him.

'You can't, Dad.' Eve's voice was shaking.

I stood up next to her and felt for her hand. 'We haven't

done anything wrong,' I said. Out of the corner of my eye I could see Mum watching us, her eyes full of worry.

Jonno clenched his fists. He looked as if he was amazed I had the audacity to speak to him.

'I want to be with Luke, Dad,' Eve said. 'I love him.'

Jonno snorted.

'You have to listen,' I said. 'There are things Eve wants. Not just me. Things like art college and stuff.'

Eve nodded. 'Things that don't include you, Dad.' Jonno stared at her.

I took a deep breath. 'And you have to accept that,' I said.

Eve squeezed my hand. I watched Jonno, my heart still beating fast. He was still staring at Eve. I suddenly saw how exhausted he was. How terrified of what we were saying. He staggered backwards.

'How about we all have a cup of tea,' Mum said shakily. She shoved a T-shirt at me and ushered me out of the room, clearly petrified Jonno was going start beating up on me again. I pulled Eve with me, past Jonno.

Eve's mum followed us downstairs. Then she and Eve had a big, weepy hug in the living room while Mum and I went into the kitchen.

Mum clattered about, filling the kettle and fetching Alice some milk from the fridge. I put on my T-shirt and leaned against the kitchen table. Gradually my hands stopped shaking. I wondered what Jonno was doing up in my room. Then thoughts of my room reminded me of last night. And Eve.

I was so lost in how amazing it had been I didn't notice Mum speaking to me until she walked over and stood right in front of me.

'Luke,' she snapped.

I focused on her. She drew in her breath, her cheeks pink. 'Anyway it's not just that I think you're too young. I won't have you bringing girls back here. It's . . . it's not on.'

I felt myself going red and slumped down at the table. 'It's not girls,' I muttered, looking down at the floor. 'It's Eve.'

'You know what I mean.'

*Yeah. I know what you mean: no sex. At least, not under my roof.*

Mum put some teabags in mugs. She bustled around the kitchen for a few minutes. Neither of us said anything. The sound of Jonno's heavy footsteps on the stairs was followed by raised voices in the living room.

I waited until the tea was ready, then took three mugs next door. Eve and her mum were on the sofa, holding hands. Jonno was sitting in Dad's armchair. He looked up briefly as I walked in. I half considered telling him to get out of my dad's chair, but decided that probably wouldn't help the situation. I set down the mugs next to the sofa and hesitated.

Eve nudged Jonno, who scowled up at me from the chair.

'Luke?' He paused. 'My daughter is demanding that I apologise to you.' He held out his hand. 'Doesn't mean I'm happy about . . . about anything,' he grunted.

He sounded as if he was still itching to punch me. I glanced at Eve. Her eyes locked on mine, urging me to go over to him. So I did. Jonno shook my outstretched hand, nodding his head curtly.

*That's the most rubbish apology I've ever had in my life.*

I said nothing.

'This doesn't mean I'm happy about the decisions Eve's making,' he blustered.

I stared at him, suddenly realising what he'd just said. He was accepting the fact that Eve had made some decisions.

'And it doesn't mean we've sorted out what's going to happen now – with where Eve lives. Or about whether she's allowed to see you. That's not sorted at all.'

He sounded stern, but there was this hollow ring to his words. I tried not to smile. He wasn't fooling me any more.

*Yeah, that is sorted, you old bastard. Because you know now that if Eve has to choose between us, she'll choose me. And you're not going to risk losing her again.*

'Right,' I said. 'Well, I'll leave you to discuss that, then.'

I backed out of the door with a final glance at Eve. Her face was composed, but her eyes were laughing. And I knew she knew exactly what I was thinking.

As I sauntered back into the kitchen, Sam started crying. Mum disappeared upstairs, coming back with him in her arms a minute later. She started heating up a bottle. Alice danced up to me, a colouring book in her hand.

'Is the pretty lady still here?' She giggled. 'Is she your girlfriend?'

I reached out and tickled her. 'Nah,' I said. 'You are.'

Then I remembered.

'Did Trisha have her baby yet?' I asked Mum.

She turned round. 'Yup,' she smiled. 'At about ten or so this morning. A boy. Nearly nine pounds. I'm taking Alice to see them both later. D'you mind watching Sam then?'

I nodded. 'Sure.'

'Thanks, love.' Mum picked up the bottle and screwed on the teat. 'Are you hungry?'

I suddenly realised that I was starving. 'Very,' I said.

Mum grinned. 'I'll do you some lunch,' she said. 'You feed the baby.' She handed me Sam and the bottle and started grilling some bacon. 'You know what I was saying earlier, Luke? About . . . you know?'

*No, Mum. Please. Do you not realise how embarrassing it is for me to discuss my sex life with you?*

'Mmmn.' I bent over the baby. He was so strong now. His little arms and legs all sturdy and his fist gripping my finger like mad. He wasn't taking the bottle though. He was looking up at me. Like he wanted to know who I was. I smiled at him. And he smiled back. A real smile.

*Wow.*

It occurred to me for the first time that it was going to be really cool having a younger brother. I could show him how to play football. And teach him stupid jokes to impress his friends with. And then, when he was older, I could tell him about girls and how to get them interested. The Six Steps Ryan had taught me – or maybe better ones . . .

I realised Mum was speaking. 'Sorry?' I looked up.

She was smiling at me. 'I was just saying how much I like Eve.' She paused and her smile grew deeper and somehow both happier and sadder at the same time. 'And you know what else?' she said. 'Your dad would have liked her very much too.'

It was all sorted pretty quickly after that. As I'd suspected, Jonno gave in on everything Eve wanted. Coming back to London to live with her mum. Even going out with me.

It was partly like I'd said – he didn't want to risk losing her again.

But it was also Eve. She'd changed so much since she ran away from Spain. The confidence I'd noticed that first evening was even stronger now – she knew exactly where she was going and what she wanted.

And what she wanted was to go back to school and apply for a place at art college to start that autumn.

Oh, yes, and me. She wanted me.

Chloe changed her job from full-time to Saturdays and went back to school too. She is the luckiest cow, you know. Really. Despite the fact that she'd missed half a term of school she still got the best results in her class in their exams. She came back home for a while, but she and Mum started arguing again, so she moved out to another cheap house-share – this one more local – and took a second job in the evenings to pay the rent.

She and Ryan are still together. Ryan suddenly got it into his head one day that he wanted to be a music agent. Says he's gonna leave school in the summer and start off by representing Cal's new band. He reckons he'll get them signed up to a record label, no problem.

Mum's getting better and better – she thinks she'll be on

her anti-depressants for a good while, but at least she's acting more normally again.

And I've got a job too – in this cool indie record shop that just opened on the high street.

I started out determined to earn enough money to buy my own guitar. Cal said that if I had my own instrument and the other guys in his new band were OK with it, I could jam with them sometimes. Maybe, eventually, play at their gigs.

First, though, it was Eve's birthday in March. I spent everything I'd made so far on buying her art stuff. Special pencils I knew she wanted and this lovely, creamy paper. Plus some frames for her best work. She's done some amazing pictures of me now. Everyone says she's really captured me.

I wonder how you do that? Sometimes I look at her sketches of me and it's the weirdest thing – I can almost tell what I was thinking when she drew me, even though I can't remember it actually happening.

Sometimes I think Eve knows me better than I know myself.

She had this little party on her birthday in March. It was great. She loved her presents. Then, later, when everyone else had gone, she said she had a present for me.

Wanna know what it was?

Cal's old guitar. She'd persuaded him to part with it for about fifty quid – most of which she still owed him – even though its worth loads more. She said he'd wanted me to have it because he thinks I've got talent.

How cool was that?

My girlfriend has a birthday.

And I get the best present.

Eve.

Always Eve.

Turn over for a taste
of the first book in
the Flynn series,
*Falling Fast*!

# 1

I stared out of the minibus window. It was raining and the pavements were a glistening grey. The houses and sky above were a softer, paler grey.

Grey. Dull. Boring. Like me. Like my life.

Maybe today would change everything.

Maybe.

Emmi peered past me. 'I think we're nearly there,' she said. 'So, River . . . you decided yet if you're gonna try for it?'

I swallowed. 'It' meant Juliet in *Romeo and Juliet*. We were on our way to auditions at St Cletus's – a local boys' secondary school that had invited Year 10s and 11s from our girls' school to try out for the female parts in the play.

Juliet was the main girl's part, of course. But that wasn't why I wanted it.

I looked out of the window again. The rain was falling harder now. I could hear it drumming on the minibus roof even over the excitable chatter inside. There were about fifteen of us, mostly girls doing drama GCSE with Ms Yates or in her after-school drama group. For everyone else, I was sure, the auditions were just a laugh.

But not to me. I wanted to be Juliet in the play, because I wanted to be Juliet in real life.

I wanted to be in love. To be loved.

I was just sixteen and I'd never met a boy I really liked. I mean, I'd met a few I quite fancied and more than a few who were fun to chat to. But I'd never felt what you could possibly describe as love. I spent a lot of time imagining it, though. Imagining what he would look like. Tall and square-jawed, I thought. With deep, soft brown eyes that would melt me with their gaze, and dark, wavy hair curling onto his neck. He wouldn't be able to take his eyes off me. We'd move towards each other like magnets. Then we would talk and talk, discovering all the things we had in common, sharing our hopes and fears and dreams. And then, finally, we would kiss. A slow, deep, romantic . . .

'Hel-lo, River.' Emmi's amused voice broke through my thoughts. 'Are you going to audition for Juliet or not?'

I glanced at Emmi's heart-shaped, dimpled face. My best friend had a sharp prettiness – all sparkling dark eyes and dramatically-long, shiny hair. Unlike me, she was relaxed and confident. She was the obvious choice for Juliet.

But I knew she was the wrong one.

Whoever played Juliet had to at least be able to imagine what it would be like to really fall in love with someone else. I was pretty sure Emmi was no more able to do that than she was to stop flirting with every guy she met.

'Don't see why not,' I shrugged, trying to look unbothered about the whole audition process. 'I mean, if you're going for a speaking part, you might as well try for all of them. Not that I really care who I end up playing.'

Emmi grinned. 'Yeah, right, Riv.'

I shrugged again and went back to the window. My face burned. Trust Emmi to have seen right through me.

The minibus was pulling into a huge, mostly empty car park. Directly in front stood a large concrete school block. It looked deserted. I checked the time on my phone. Four p.m.

'Guess all the boys have gone home,' Emmi said. She sounded disappointed.

'Good.' I stood up and joined the queue to get off the minibus. 'The last thing we need is an audience.'

Emmi laughed. 'Isn't an audience exactly what we're here for?'

We got off the minibus and milled awkwardly in the car park. The rain had lightened to a soft drizzle. The absolute worst kind of weather for my hair, which gets all frizzy at the first sign of moisture.

A tall, very thin man with a high forehead and slicked back dark hair came striding towards us. A boy in the St Cletus school uniform of black trousers, white shirt and black-and-green striped tie trotted awkwardly beside him.

Ms Yates smiled nervously. 'That's Mr Nichols, the head of drama,' she said.

'Hello there,' the man boomed. For such a thin person, his voice was surprisingly deep. 'I'm Mr Nichols. Welcome to St Cletus's.' He beamed round at us all, casting a particularly warm smile at Ms Yates. 'Now let's get you in out of the rain.' He flung his arms out to indicate the boy beside him. 'If anyone needs the bathroom, James Molloy here will show you to the Ladies.'

Fifteen pairs of eyes swivelled to look at James Molloy.

He had sandy-coloured hair and a squishy, comfortable face. Underneath the flush of embarrassment creeping up his cheeks, I could see he looked nice. Nice, as in open and friendly.

You can't fall in love with nice.

Mr Nichols strode off towards the school building, indicating – with another exaggerated arm movement – that we should follow.

We all scuttled after him.

James Molloy had – surprise, surprise – gravitated almost immediately to Emmi's side.

'Hi,' he said hopefully, then blushed.

Emmi flashed him a big smile. 'Hi,' she purred. 'I'm Emmi.'

I giggled.

James Molloy gulped. He looked as if he was desperately trying to think of something to say.

We reached the large wooden door that Mr Nichols had just walked through. James held it open to let Emmi past, then dived after her, ahead of me.

'We're going to the sixth form common room,' he said. 'The auditions'll be in there.'

Emmi glanced over her shoulder and cocked an eyebrow at him. 'Will boys be watching?' she said in a silky voice.

She was really turning it on, but I could tell it was all for effect. Emmi liked to know that she could have any boy she wanted, but I'd never seen her bothered about any of them. Any other girl would have been labelled a slag, but Emmi somehow got away with it.

Poor James Molloy's face was now the colour of a tomato.

'Er . . . no,' he stammered. 'That is, not until the second round. Mr Nichols asked for people with main parts to stay after school to read with some of the girls when he's heard you all.'

'Ah . . .' Emmi said knowingly.

God, that meant having to do bits of the play with boys later. I glanced at Emmi. How come she wasn't in the slightest bit nervous about that?

'So the boys' parts are already cast?' Grace asked timidly.

Grace is my other really good friend. She's completely different from Emmi: shy and quiet . . . and she's been going out with the same guy for, like, forever.

James nodded, then led us along a series of chilly, rather rundown corridors, into a common room, complete with a pool table, a row of lockers and some bright red sofas.

'Please take off your coats and make yourselves comfortable.' Mr Nichols' booming voice resonated around its bare walls

'Sixth form common room,' James announced unnecessarily, staring at a patch of skin a few centimetres to the left of Emmi's nose.

Emmi nodded vaguely and wandered across the room. I turned to James.

'What part are you playing?' I said.

'Mercutio.' He blushed. 'Romeo's best friend. Which is cool, because the guy playing Romeo *is* my best friend.'

His eyes drifted sideways to where Emmi was self-consciously twisting her long hair in her hand. I watched his gaze flickering over Emmi's tall, slim body. She always seemed to manage to have her skirt a few centimetres higher than everyone else. She also wore her sweater tighter and her blouse unbuttoned further. When she walked she wiggled her bum and flashed off legs that went up to her armpits.

My heart sank. No way was I getting the part of Juliet instead of her. Not unless the guy playing Romeo was really short and Mr Nichols was practically blind.

I knew I should have been pleased for Emmi, but I wanted this so badly and I didn't stand a chance.

'Emmi's my best friend,' I said confidingly.

James Molloy looked down at me. For a second I saw myself through his eyes: I was short. I was dumpy. I was – *God*, I was like him. Squishy and comfortable.

At that point two other girls skittered over in fits of giggles and asked James to show them where the toilets were.

They all disappeared and I went to find Emmi and Grace.

'I'm so nervous,' Grace squeaked.

'For God's sake, Grace,' Emmi drawled. 'All you're doing is reciting a short poem. The worst that can happen is you'll end up a townsperson of Verona.'

Grace looked a little deflated. I don't think Emmi means it, but sometimes she can sound a bit harsh. After all, Grace was mostly here to support me and Emmi. Sure, she was doing drama GCSE, but performing wasn't really her thing.

I smiled at her. 'You'll be fine,' I said. 'You look really pretty.'

Grace smiled gratefully back at me. 'You look lovely too, Riv. I wish I had a figure like yours.' She sighed, then ran her fingers through her soft, strawberry blonde waves. 'And your hair really works the way you've got it tied back like that. You're so lucky it's so thick.'

*Yeah, right.* She was just being polite. Did I mention I have horrible frizzy hair and as for my body . . . well, maybe I'd look okay if I could lose half a stone . . . but however hard I tried, the weight never came off.

'Er . . . thanks, Grace.'

Emmi yawned. 'I don't know what you're getting anxious about,' she said to Grace. 'It'll be over soon, then you can phone Darren and tell him all about it.'

'Darren said he didn't like the idea of me being in a play at a boys' school,' Grace said.

Emmi rolled her eyes. 'Well, that's his problem, isn't it?'

I squeezed Grace's hand sympathetically, but the truth was I had no idea what Grace saw in Darren. He was geeky and spotty – while Grace was sweetly pretty, with her wide blue eyes and perfect skin. Plus, I was pretty sure he didn't have a passionate bone in his body. Mind you, looking at Grace's pale, anxious face, I wasn't sure she did either.

The thought depressed me. It seemed entirely possible Grace would go through her whole life never feeling an overwhelming, die-for-you love.

Lots of people probably didn't.

*Not me, though. Please. Not me.*

I closed my eyes and tried to remember the lines I'd picked for my audition.

The room fell silent. Mr Nichols cleared his throat.

'I think we'll start with a simple visualisation,' he said. 'Please, everyone, find a space to stand, then close your eyes and imagine a busy marketplace in old Verona. Observe the bustle, the townspeople in their long gowns, all going about their business. Take time to smell the freshly baked bread, to squeeze the soft fruits on the stalls, to feel the warm sun on your back . . .' He droned on.

I sighed. This was exactly the sort of rubbish Ms Yates was into. I let my mind drift back to my ideal guy.

A minute or two later and Mr Nichols made us visualise walking into the centre of the marketplace and sitting in a circle on the ground.

'Now if you'd all open your eyes and find a seat . . . we'll start the auditions by going round the room,' he said.

There was a scramble for seats. I found myself perched on the arm of a sofa, next to Emmi.

'Okay, let's get going,' Mr Nichols said, suddenly brisk and businesslike. 'Please give your name before you begin.' He looked over to the door. 'James, tell the boys we'll be up in about half an hour. And shut the door on your way out.'

With a swift glance at Emmi's elegantly crossed legs, James backed out of the door. We all looked at Mr Nichols.

'A volunteer to start?' he said.

Everyone looked at their laps. Then I felt Emmi raise her hand beside me. 'I don't mind going first,' she said.

She sashayed over to the open space in the middle of the room. She faced Mr Nichols and smiled – a coy, shy smile. God, she hadn't even started and she was already acting.

Ms Yates nodded approvingly. She, like most of our teachers, loved Emmi because she was always prepared to speak out in class and because she was polite – at least to the teachers' faces.

She did a speech from the play – the beginning of the scene where Juliet is on her balcony and Romeo sneaks over to talk to her. She was good ... She moved around naturally, and put loads of expression into her voice. But for all that, she never really sounded like she meant anything she was saying. I watched Mr Nichols. He was concentrating intently on her, his eyes following her as she moved. At the end she looked up at him from under her eyelashes. He nodded and smiled at Ms Yates.

*Great.*

After that we went clockwise round the room. Grace was next. Unlike Emmi she didn't move into the middle of the room. Instead, she stood where she was and recited her poem in a loud, clear voice.

She was actually quite good. A bit stiff maybe, but she put loads of expression into what she was saying and at least she remembered all the words. Asha Watkins forgot her poem, while Maisie Holtwood refused to even start. Two more girls just stood there, staring shyly at the carpet as they did a bit from the play.

On and on it went. After twenty minutes Mr Nichols was looking bored, his chin propped in his hands. A sly smile was sneaking across Emmi's lips. So far there was no one to touch her.

Thanks to the order we were sitting in, my audition was going to be last. I tried not to let the wait prey on my nerves.

A few more girls gave okay-ish performances. Daisy Walker, a tall girl with high cheekbones and intense dark eyes, was good. She moved about a bit, using her hands expressively like Emmi had done.

I felt more and more nervous. The time dragged and dragged. Then suddenly it speeded up and Mr Nichols' eyes were on mine – 'Yes?' he said.

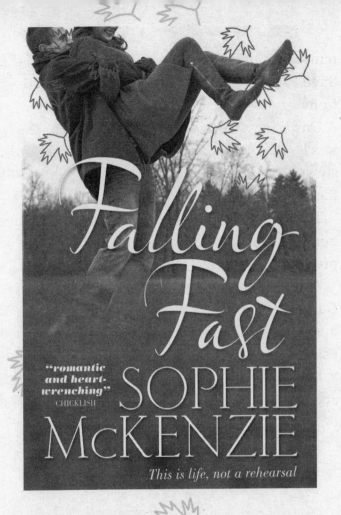

# Falling Fast

## SOPHIE McKENZIE

"romantic and heart-wrenching"
CHICKLISH

*This is life, not a rehearsal*

When River auditions for a part in an inter-school performance of Romeo and Juliet, she finds herself smitten by Flynn, the boy playing Romeo. River believes in romantic love, and she can't wait to experience it. But Flynn comes from a damaged family - is he even capable of giving River what she wants? The path of true love never did run smooth...

ISBN 978-0-85707-099-9 £6.99

"romantic
and heart-
wrenching"
CHICKLISH
on Falling Fast

*Burning*
*Bright*

SOPHIE
McKENZIE

*Should love really be this intense?*

Four months have passed and River and Flynn's
romance is still going strong. River thinks Flynn has
his anger under control, but when she discovers he
has been getting into fights and is facing a terrible
accusation at school, she starts to question both
Flynn's honesty - and the intensity of their passion.
Things come to a head at a family get together
when River sees Flynn fly into one unprovoked
rage too many. The consequences for both of them
are devastating and threaten to tear them apart
forever.

ISBN 978-0-85707-101-9 £6.99

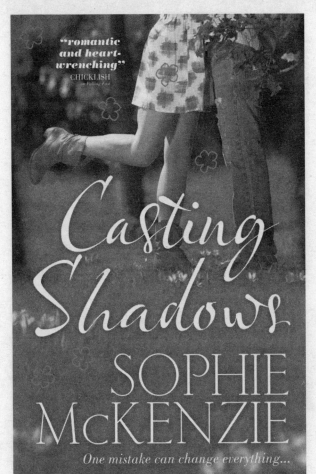

"romantic and heart-wrenching"
CHICKLISH
on *Falling Fast*

*Casting*
*Shadows*

SOPHIE
McKENZIE

*One mistake can change everything...*

Flynn is making every effort to stay in control of his hot temper, while River feels more content than she's ever been. Together the two of them make big plans for the future, but powerful secrets lurk in the shadows, ready to threaten their happiness.

ISBN 978-0-85707-103-3 £6.99

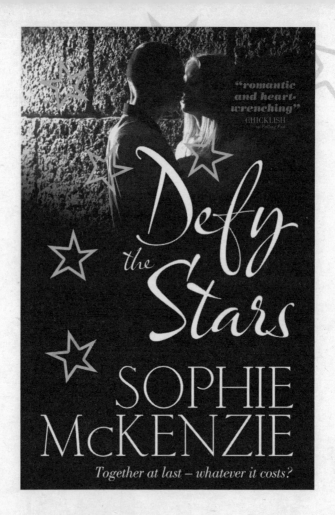

"romantic
and heart-
wrenching"
CHICKLISH
on Falling Fast

*Defy*
*the*
*Stars*

SOPHIE
McKENZIE

*Together at last – whatever it costs?*

After months apart, everyone thinks that River
is successfully building a future without Flynn.
Indeed, she has almost convinced herself that she
is moving on. And then, one day, Flynn is back,
bringing with him tales of his glamorous new life.
River suspects his lucrative new work involves
some form of criminal activity, but will she let
herself be drawn back into Flynn's world? Or is
this, finally, the end of the line for them both?

ISBN 978-0-85707-105-7 £6.99